The Meditating Mother
and Other Stories

The Meditating Mother
and Other Stories

by Laura Kopchick

For Meadow —
I hope you enjoy
these stories.
Happy Reading!
Laura Kopchick

Copyright 2023 @ Lamar University Literary Press
All Rights Reserved

ISBN: 978-1-962148-15-3
Library of Congress Control Number: 2024949129

Editor: Kelsey Leger

Lamar University Literary Press
Beaumont, TX

The author wishes to express deep gratitude to the editors and readers of the following publications where the stories below first appeared:

Potomac Review: Fall 2018, Issue 63: "The Monkey Woman Who Married the Alligator Boy Makes A Comeback"

Archaeopteryx: Fall 2012: "The Meditating Mother"

Ascent: Fall 2002: "The Other Dorothy"

Santa Monica Review: Fall 1997: "Leaving"

Recent Prose by Lamar University Literary Press

Robert Bonazzi, *Awakened by Surprise*
David Bowles, *Border Lore: Folktales and Legends of South Texas*
Kevin K. Casey, *Four-Peace*
Terry Dalrymple, *Love Stories (Sort of)*
Gerald Duff, *Legends of Lost Man Marsh*
Britt Haraway, *Early Men*
Michael Howarth, *Fair Weather Ninjas*
Gretchen Johnson, *The Joy of Deception*
Tom Mack & Andrew Geyer, *A Shared Voice*
Carl Parker, *Turtle on a Post*
Moumin Quazi, *Migratory Words*
Harold Raley, *Lost River Anthology*
Harold Raley, *Louisiana Rogue*
Jim Sanderson, *Trashy Behavior*
Jan Seale, *A Lifetime of Words*
Jan Seale, *Appearances*
Jan Seale, *Ordinary Charms*
C.W. Smith, *The Museum of Marriage*
Melvin Sterne, *The Number You Have Reached*
Melvin Sterne, *Redemption*
Melvin Sterne, *The Shoeshine Boy*
John Wegner, *Love Is Not a Dirty Word*

CONTENTS

The Meditating Mother..9

Breaking the Neighbors...23

Small Bursts of Kindness..39

The Monkey Woman Who Married the Alligator
Boy Makes A Comeback...55

Jimmy and Mary at Home Plate..67

Leaving..81

Krum, Texas..93

Bigger Than Love...109

The Other Dorothy...123

Cicadas..141

For Tim and Harper and Ben

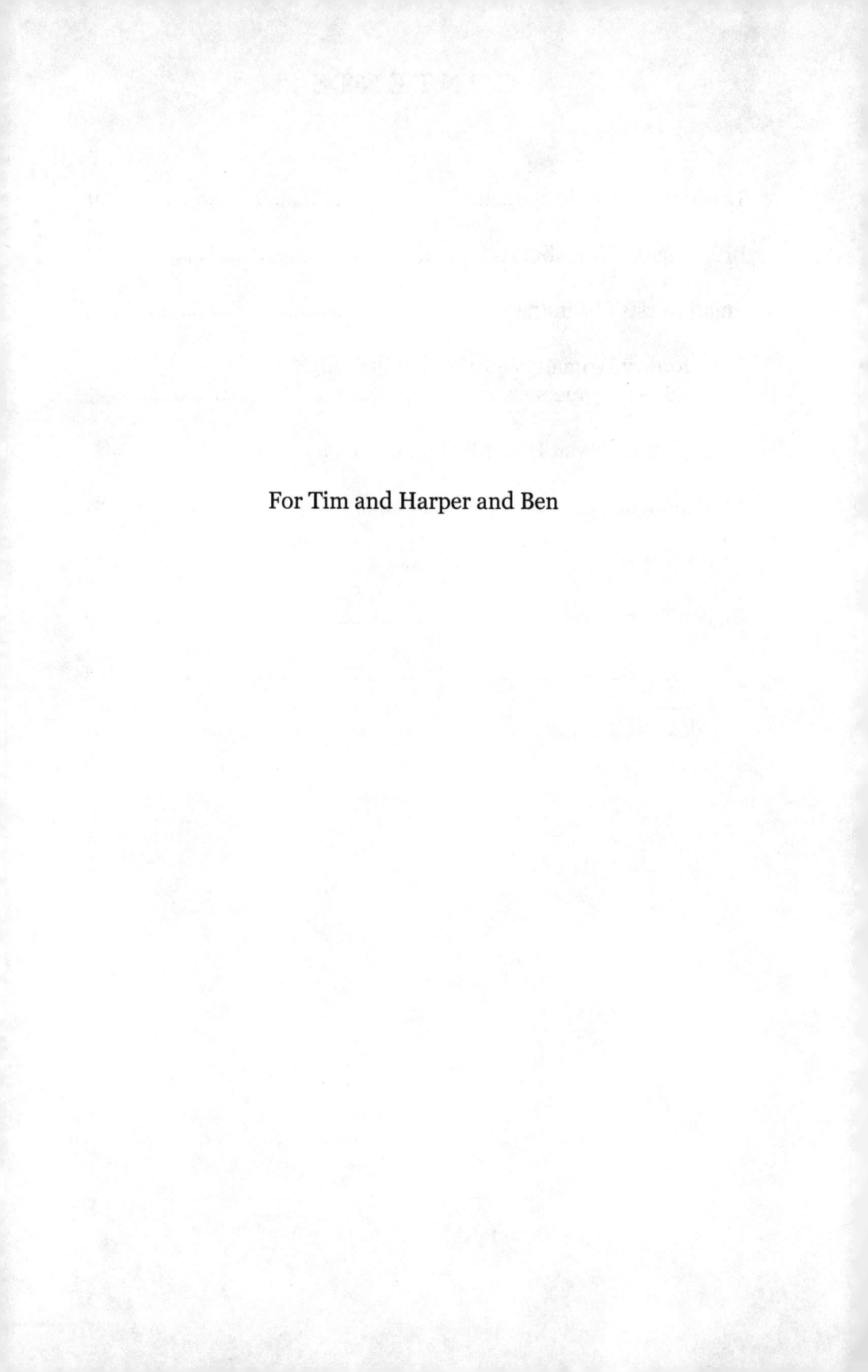

The Meditating Mother

The Mother started the drug chant alphabetically, with *Captopril*, her voice a low monotone, and Stella turned to look at the blurred outline of the woman's body, which she could see too clearly through the filmy curtain. The Mother sat cross-legged on the bed behind her baby's crib, arms resting on her knees, hands held palm up as if she were meditating. *Captopril*. The Mother repeated the word, rounding the vowels and blurring the consonants until the letters came together in a measured cadence. Later she added *Digoxin, Lasix, Potassium, Prostoglandin.*

"What's wrong with him, do you think?" Stella asked Nate. The surgical team had moved the woman's son into the ICU late in the afternoon and the Mother had been sitting on the pull-out couch behind her son's crib since the nurse had set up his oxygen and explained how to care for his feeding tube. Stella's daughter, Gracie, had a feeding tube and they'd received the same scripted instructions. Gracie had been in the Pediatric Cardiology ICU for three days now and refused to eat. Instead, she pursed her lips against the strange rubber nipple. The first two days in the ICU Nate had remained silent on Gracie's refusal of the formula, and on Stella's sudden milk stoppage, until earlier that morning when Dr. Tam mentioned putting Gracie on steroids. All day Nate watched the clock above Gracie's crib and nodded his head toward the nursing room every couple of hours.

Crammed together on the pull-out bed behind Gracie's crib, Stella's back rested against Nate's warm stomach and his breathing settled into a pattern that told her he was on the verge of sleep.

"He's worse than Gracie," Nate said.

"All those drugs," Stella said. "All those drop-ins from Dr. Tam." Stella knew Dr. Tam only dropped in on the serious cases—the ones Gracie's nurse called "wait and see's."

She thought of getting away from Dr. Tam and moving out of the ICU, into one of the private rooms up on the sixth floor. Up there they'd be able to watch their own TV and sleep on a nice-sized flip-out couch and Gracie would have a normal crib, one with sides like the one she had at home. On the tour before the surgery, it became clear—without the hospitality guide having to tell them—that when a baby moved upstairs, everything would turn out okay.

After Gracie's surgery, when they first moved her into the ICU, the baby next to Gracie's station—the station the Meditating Mother's baby now occupied—was being put into a red plastic wagon, his heart monitor balanced in front of him on a pile of blankets. The boy, gauze cleanly taped to his chest, happily tapped his hand against the side of the wagon, and his father, a young Mexican man, had clapped and played peek-a-boo with his son while the nurses packed up all of the stuffed animals and family photographs that filled his area. "Upstairs today," the man had said to Stella. Then he pointed up at the ceiling as if he didn't trust his English, and Stella had nodded her head and pulled the curtain around Gracie's crib.

Stella lay with one leg over the edge of the bed, nearly touching Gracie's elevated crib. *Digoxin*, Stella thought. *Lasix*. The expensive pink diaper bag, covered in a shiny plastic material already torn at the corners, rested on the floor near Stella's arm. In the soft, green illumination from the monitor's glow, she could see Gracie's wooden rattle in the shape of a flower, with its tiny gold cluster of bells at the center of the petals. Gracie couldn't hold the wooden hoop securely in her fingers yet, but she liked to pull the flower to her mouth and nurse the bells. The empty bottle with the miniature giraffes marching in a line around the surface, chasing day-glo butterflies, rested in the small pouch on the side of the bag. One of the nurses had told Stella and Nate to bring Gracie's favorite toy as a comfort to her after the surgery and Stella had swallowed the fact that Gracie didn't yet have a favorite toy.

The Mother's son's monitor rested on a cart behind the thin striped curtain at the foot of Nate and Stella's pull-out bed and gave off a steady pattern of two short bursts and then one long one. Stella tapped this rhythm with her fingertips against the knobby bones of Nate's knuckle on the hand that he had resting against her stomach and repeated the woman's chant over and over in her head, imagining how it would feel to say the words out loud. Saying the names of the drugs in her head kept her from thinking about the wire now attached to the outside of Gracie's heart, or the tape they had put over her eyes before the surgery, or how four days earlier, on the night before Nate and Stella had brought her to the hospital, they had dressed Gracie up like a baby chick for her first Easter and she had picked at the yellow and orange striped tights with her fingertips.

"I feel sorry for that woman," Stella said. She tried not to think about Dr. Tam, about the way the long black hairs crept up and around his thick gold wedding ring. When Stella had asked him how Gracie's surgery had gone, an hour or so after they'd moved her into the ICU, he'd paused longer than necessary and said, "Fine." When she asked about the delay he'd been worried about in what he'd told them was called her QT interval, he said, "We'll know more when she's off the feeding tube and oxygen." Then he turned and revealed a gold-capped bicuspid when he smiled at the representative from the pacemaker company who was there to explain to them how Gracie's remote Carelink monitor worked.

"What about the baby?" Nate said, loudly enough that they heard the Mother shift around on her bed. "He's the one with the hole in his heart, or whatever it is they can't fix."

"He's just a baby," Stella said. "He won't remember any of this. She will."

Nate pushed himself up on his elbow and rested his chin on Stella's shoulder. He smelled sour, the way Gracie smelled when she hadn't had a bath in a few days and the milk settled into the creases in her neck. Stella turned her face toward him, longing to smell Gracie now, though she smelled nothing like she did at home. Each hour in this Intensive Care Unit diluted the smell of her—as if her daughter were dissolving into the grief that had settled in this room. Stella wanted Gracie home, dressed in her velour pink onesie, her dark eyes widening whenever the cat sprung onto the windowsill.

When Stella sat up and slid her feet into her slippers, she didn't tell Nate about her need to smell their baby. Stella had gone to Gracie's crib twice already tonight, each time waking her up and making her pull at the wires of her monitor. Instead, she said, "Pump, pump, pump. I feel like a cow." Stella's breasts ached, and her left one had grown hard. For six months she had nursed Gracie, never giving her a bottle. The professional pump in the small room off of the Pediatric Cardiac Intensive Care Unit could pump both breasts at one time, but in the fluorescent lighting, the machine looked alien and precise—like something from a science fiction movie.

"Go," Nate said. "I'll listen for her." He rubbed Stella's arm and then let his hand slip to the side of her waist, where her hip bone would be if she had already lost the baby weight. They had both grown doughy since her pregnancy, their bones now buried deep beneath the soft surface of their skin.

"Okay, but don't fall asleep," she said. "How can you sleep?"

Nate's chest deflated as he exhaled. "Let that milk flow," he finally said. He rubbed her side and Stella's skin went numb there, as if Nate were actually capable of erasing the feeling from her body.

"We'll never move upstairs," she said. "I don't think upstairs really exists."

Nate shifted in the small bed, already claiming her side as his own. "Go," he said and gave her a light push. "May the Milking Gods be with you." He sounded half asleep already, the end of his sentence disappearing into the thin foam of his pillow.

In front of Stella, behind the curtain at the foot of their bed, the Meditating Mother coughed. The sound came from deep in her chest, where some infection had rooted itself and wouldn't let go.

Nate and Stella had found out about Gracie's heart defect eight days earlier, on a routine trip to a cardiologist to check out what the pediatrician had called "a gentle murmur with a musical quality" and when she'd said this, Stella had thought of a little cartoon guitar in the shape of a heart with the strings being plucked. But at the cardiologist's, as the doctor moved the stethoscope around Gracie's small chest, one edge of her diaper slipping loose, Stella noticed the slow, deliberate way the doctor pushed the scope over her daughter's skin and her throat closed up. The cardiologist, a woman with a mess of curly, dark hair and thin arms with small, knotty muscles, had kept them waiting too long after Gracie's heart ultrasound. Now she avoided looking at them, instead focusing her attention on Gracie's chest, nimbly navigating the minefield of electrode patches that littered her small body.

"I'm not an electrical specialist," she finally said. She pulled the stethoscope from around her neck and stood up, then she looked at Nate and pulled a drawing from the pocket of her white lab coat. The drawing looked like a simple ink sketch of a heart from a fifth-grade science book. The cardiologist positioned her red pen over the drawing and drew arrows and lines and explained that Gracie's heart had no electrical current going from the top chamber to the bottom.

"Her prognosis will depend on the surgery, which has its risks, and how her body responds to the pacemaker. But the electrical cardiologist will go over that information with you, and so will the surgeon." *Electrical Cardiologist. Surgeon.* Stella took hold of Gracie's hand, which she was using to swipe the doctor's stethoscope. The red arrows drawn over the cheap photocopied heart made Stella think of a Frieda Kahlo painting she had seen at the Art Institute when she had taken Nate's mother there over Christmas.

They took the train home. Stella sat with Gracie pushed against her chest and tried to call her mom on her cell phone. She couldn't get reception, though, and even if she had, the noise from the grinding tracks beneath them would have made conversation impossible. Everyone around her—Nate, the teenager with the iPod and the braided hair, the Mexican woman holding a blonde-haired infant—looked at her once, maybe twice, then pretended not to notice what was obvious. Finally, Nate reached over and put his hand against Gracie's back. Gracie let out a small "Da," and then put her lips together to blow spit bubbles. Her white collar was spotted a light brown from the strained peaches she had had for lunch. The hair at the back of her head had started to grow, finally, into light brown waves that Stella pushed her fingers through.

"We should have taken the car," Stella said. She rubbed Gracie's back and thought of the heart drawing that she had stuffed into her purse after the cardiologist left it in the examination room, along with Gracie's paperwork.

Nate pulled his hand away. "Expensive parking," he finally said. Stella looked at him and studied his face, soft and pink from the heat inside the train. When the train lurched at the Belmont stop, Nate wiped his face before he reached over and put his hand on top of Stella's. "It's okay," he said. "It's going to be okay."

After thirty minutes of pumping, Stella deposited the nearly empty plastic bag in the storage cooler at the end of the ICU and walked across the hall to the women's restroom. There was a row of toilets on one end and a row of sinks and shower stalls on the other. The grey tiles were speckled with dark spots, which Stella at first had mistaken for an infestation of ants. At the end of the room, at the farthest sink, the Meditating Mother stood staring into the mirror, the water running in the sink in front of her. Stella stared at the back of the Mother's neck, at the pale strip of skin that cut underneath the harsh line of her black bobbed hair.

When the Mother saw Stella, she turned away from the mirror and stared at her. "Your baby's awake," she said. "I called your nurse." The Mother's voice sounded different—higher-pitched, louder—than when she chanted her incantation in the language of drugs. Stella thought of the neat row of nearly empty milk bags in the cooler, and then of Nate, asleep on the pull-out bed, his mouth open.

"Thank you," Stella said. Then, because she felt that she needed to say something else, "My husband is exhausted."

The Meditating Mother turned off the water and faced the mirror again. "They don't understand what it's like," she said. "They don't have the same connection that we do." She said this firmly and for some reason, Stella started to cry. Maybe she wasn't using the machine correctly. Maybe she should ask one of the nurses to help her. Or Nate. Maybe Nate should go into the room with her and deal with the tubes and suction cups. Stella hadn't cried since they brought Gracie down the hall for surgery, and now she leaned back against the cool, grey tile and let the chill ease its way into her skin. She wanted to wash her face, her hair. She wanted to get into one of the shower stalls and drench herself with cool water. She wanted to make herself disappear.

"Stop that," the Meditating Mother said, and when Stella looked up she saw that the woman was speaking to her. "Go in there and take care of her," she said. "You're one of the lucky ones." She turned away from Stella again and turned on the water, then leaned over the sink and spread her open palms under the spout.

Stella thought of the thick silver staples in her daughter's chest, of the gauzy white tape that had held her daughter's eyes closed during her surgery. The empty milk sacks that kept Gracie in the ICU. "I'm sorry."

"What for?" the Meditating Mother said. Water dripped from her pale face, spotting the lavender nightgown she wore.

"I don't know," Stella said. "I'm just sorry."

"Well don't be," the Mother said. She wiped her hands on the front of her nightgown and walked past Stella to leave. She smelled like all of the mothers in the ICU—a mixture of sharp disinfectant and rose-scented soap.

In the ICU, the fluorescent light spotlighted Gracie's chest incision; a nurse stood over her crib, trying to coax her into taking a bottle. Nate stood next to the nurse, his arm resting next to Gracie's feeding tube. The nurse's white face mask made her look as if she were some nameless horror with no mouth, yet capable still of devouring Gracie's arms and legs, her swollen cheeks. When Nate saw Stella, he smiled. The nurse paused and waited for Stella to walk across the room, past the Meditating Mother's boy, whose skin seemed translucent in the pool of halogen where he slept.

The nurse handed Stella the bottle and then looked down at Gracie's chart, which she held in front of her, carefully, like an undecipherable calculus. Stella tilted the bottle and rubbed the nipple against Gracie's lower lip, just as the nurse had shown her. Some milk pooled in the crevice of Gracie's closed lips, which were chapped and pink.

"Open your lips, Muffin," Stella whispered. She moved the bottle back and forth, slowly, and Gracie turned her head away. Finally, without opening her eyes, Gracie parted her lips and Stella slid the nipple, which was an obscene aqua blue—the color of cupcake frosting—into her mouth. Gracie sucked in her cheeks, swallowing twice, before tasting the rubber and pushing the nipple out with her tongue. She squeezed her eyes and clenched her tiny fists.

Later, when Gracie had fallen back asleep and Stella came back to bed, Nate put his arm around her. "Any luck pumping?" he asked, as if all she had to do was rub a rabbit's foot and her milk would magically flow.

"Maybe we should hook *you* up to that thing and see how you do," she said.

"I don't think I'd have much luck," Nate said. "I'm a B-cup at best." Then, when she wouldn't let him touch her, he said, "So I fell asleep, I'm sorry. I'm tired."

Stella let him slip his arm around her. "Well I am, too."

"We both are," he said. "Right?"

Nate moved in close to her and then leaned down to tug at the tangled bedsheet. Later, Stella fell asleep with his hand resting against the small of her back, listening to the Meditating Mother on the other side of the curtain. She had started chanting again, going through the list of words that sounded like foreign countries, ready to be invaded. *Captopril, Digoxin, Lasix, Potassium, Prostoglandin.*

The next morning, the nurses pulled open the curtains and raised the lights enough to read the charts. The babies—all in the same transparent cribs without side panels—mostly slept while the parents rubbed the small muscles in their legs and took turns going to the bathroom or down to the cafeteria. Each baby had a day nurse, and Gracie's nurse was a youngish woman, probably a few years out of college, with long red hair. She was noticeably pregnant, the top of her scrubs outfit straining across her wide stomach. On Gracie's first day in the ICU, she had told Nate and Stella that she'd demanded to have a 3-D heart ultrasound of her baby.

"I can take Down Syndrome, but I've been working here long enough to know I can't take a heart problem." She fussed with the tape that held Gracie's breathing tube in place.

Lucky us, Stella had wanted to say. Instead, she said, "I bet this place gets depressing," and watched as the nurse's plump fingers felt around the gauze taped over Gracie's chest, and then the other, smaller piece that covered the pacemaker wound on her abdomen. Stella remembered the fuzzy yellow body of the chicken costume and the small wings that stuck out and made Gracie look like she had no arms.

"You have no idea." The nurse sounded exhausted, and she reached her hand to rub her own belly the way all pregnant mothers do without even thinking about it, and Stella found herself touching her own belly, too, trying to remember the feeling of all of those sharp angles—a fist or an elbow or a heel—pushing out against her skin and then rolling away inward, to take a jab at the ribs.

While Stella waited for Dr. Tam to come check Gracie's fluid levels, Nate went down the hall to the family waiting center, which someone had decided to decorate with brightly carpeted walls and permanent wooden play structures, miniaturized for indoors. Along one wall stood a row of computers, separated by metal privacy panels. The few times Stella had been to the room she'd avoided the computers and instead sat with a cup of coffee and watched a half hour of morning television. The bright television hosts perked up in their Spring pastel suits, became for her proof that the world outside of the hospital had continued, without machines that pumped and whined and suctioned off fluids. Had continued without sutures and sideless cribs.

When Nate returned he paused by the glass doors and sanitized his hands with the gel that seemed to disappear on contact, then came up behind Stella as she stood over Gracie.

"She looks good." He touched Gracie's small shoulder.

"You'll wake her. Stop it."

Gracie's eyelids fluttered and Nate moved his hand and touched her cheek. "Bottle," Nate whispered to Gracie. "When you wake up, you're going to drink from a bottle."

"Fat chance," Stella said.

"We could get her one of those helmets with the drink holders," Nate said. "Like we saw at the Cubs game." He leaned his chin against Stella's shoulder and squeezed the side of his face against hers. He smelled like soap—he'd snuck a quick shower in the men's room across the hall. Stella had promised herself that she wouldn't take one until they got upstairs and Gracie could finally bathe, too, safely tucked away in the privacy of their own room, her body free from the machines and the feeding tubes. The curls at the back of her head had gone limp from four straight days in the crib.

Gracie stretched one arm out and then made a grimace. When she tried to cry, her mouth stayed open but no sound came out.

Stella wanted to pick her up, feel Gracie's weight against her chest, and run her fingers over the soft, downy hair on top of her head that felt, to Stella, like nothing else she had ever touched. But when Stella's eyes started to water, she thought instead of the alien pumping machine, and of the row of flat milk bags. Maybe if she put all of the bags together and Gracie drank most of the milk, that would be enough for Dr. Tam. If she could get Gracie through one good feeding with a bottle by the time Dr. Tam came up for his afternoon rounds, maybe he'd let Gracie go.

"She looks like a doll," Stella said. She wasn't used to seeing Gracie in only a diaper, her small shoulders rounded and soft. Without the clothes, the pink ribbons and polka dots, Gracie seemed on the verge of disappearing and there would be nothing to prove she had ever existed at all. Stella touched the dark bruise that had formed on Gracie's side, next to her ribs, near the small hole the surgeons cut for a drainage tube. The Meditating Mother was right—Nate didn't want to scream at the doctors for putting a hole in the side of his daughter's body, or for breaking her breastbone to attach wires to her tiny fist of a heart. He didn't want to slam the heart monitor into the wall and run screaming down the hall, destroying everything man-made in an incandescent rage. Stella did.

The nurse had come up behind Stella and rolled the IV cart away from Gracie's crib. She held a full IV bag in one hand and a roll of gauze in the other. "Time for a change," she said.

Stella turned to Nate. "There's probably three ounces in the cooler if you combine the bags," she said, turning her back to Gracie's crib so she wouldn't have to see the small staples that worked their way up Gracie's chest, and the row of dark stitches that zipped up between them.

Stella thought of Nate's jokes about all of the tattoos Gracie would eventually cover her chest with, anyway, when she turned into a rebellious teenager who stalked the malls. She thought of all of the jokes Nate had made over the past four days, which Stella knew were meant to cheer her up, but instead made Stella want to slap him, hard. Make him blink as his eyes teared up, make him realize that this—whatever this was—would never be something to make light of, not ever. Not even if they suddenly woke to discover it was just a nightmare they'd somehow sleepwalked into, could it ever be recalled without horror and anguish. She looked at his fleshy white cheek. Nate must have seen this violence in her face because instead of making a comment about how happy he had been the last time someone offered him three ounces of something, or instead of making another joke about breasts, he just turned and took the bottle from the diaper bag and headed for the refrigerator at the end of the room, his gaze focused on the wall in front of him. Not on the row of cribs and curtains and mothers.

As soon as Stella opened the door, she heard the grinding hum of the pumping machine.

"Come in," the Meditating Mother said. "I'm almost finished." The Mother sat on an overstuffed loveseat against the wall, with her blouse with tiny blue flowers unbuttoned, the machine sitting against the wall across the room from her, pumping air. The Mother sighed and leaned back, her shirt spreading open to reveal her small white breasts.

"I can come back," Stella said and started to turn away from her.

"Sit," the Mother said. She patted the cushion next to her and Stella sat, so close that Stella's thigh touched hers. Unlike Stella's breasts, which strained against her nursing bra, the Mother's looked incapable of producing anything. In the harsh fluorescent lights, Stella now realized that the bobbed haircut had grown out too much and was plagued with split ends. Up close, Stella could tell the woman was older than she'd originally thought—maybe in her mid-forties. She thought of all of the older women at her obstetrician's office who would cautiously ask to touch her swollen belly, their own stomachs flat and smooth in their pencil skirts and wrap dresses. "I never get anything, anyway," the Meditating Mother said. "But I try." The Mother held the plastic bag in her hand, her baby's patient sticker lopsided across the top. "I thought I'd do better with their pump." She looked down at the bag in her lap and then looked up at Stella. "How many days have you been here? Three?"

"Today is day four," Stella said. The sound of the pump made it difficult to speak quietly, so Stella got up to turn it off.

"Go ahead and pump," the Meditating Mother said. "Don't mind me."

Stella sat down in the hard chair in the corner next to the pump and opened up her shirt and the flaps of her nursing bra, which even Nate hadn't seen her do. At home, she always took the baby into their bedroom and shut the door. The skin felt hard and hot underneath her fingers and Stella winced as she moved to position the pump's cup over her breast.

"No wonder," the woman said.

When Stella looked up, she could see the woman staring at her chest, then she pointed at Stella's breast. "You've got an infection." She dropped her hand and stood up, then came over and leaned down to look more closely at Stella's breast, which was bright red. The Meditating Mother touched her cool palm against the skin next to Stella's nipple. "I'm going to get you a heating pad," she said. "But what you really need is cabbage leaves."

"Cabbage leaves," Stella repeated.

The Mother ignored her remark and instead moved her hand up to press the back of her hand against Stella's forehead, then her cheek. The Mother's skin felt papery and thin, like the outside peels of an onion.

"Don't worry," the Mother said. She stood up and helped Stella position the pump's suction cup over her swollen breast. "See if you can get anything," the Mother said. "I'll be back in a minute."

The Mother left before Stella could remind her to button her shirt, and Stella imagined the Mother bumping into Dr. Tam in the hallway, his eyes looking discreetly away as he brushed past her on his way to the ICU.

On the morning of her surgery, the surgeon who would crack open Gracie's chest and screw the leads of the pacemaker to the surface of her heart had come into the pre-op room to ask Stella and Nate if they had any questions before Gracie was wheeled to the operating room down the hall, behind two white double doors with no windows. Stella stared at the surgeon's clogs, which weren't white but a dark brown and so worn that a hole had formed over the big toe on one of them.

"What does it look like?" Stella asked.

The surgeon had crossed his arms, confused. "What does what look like?"

"The pacemaker," Stella said. Gracie lay on the examining table, playing with her rattle. She turned to look at Stella, her brown eyes cloudy from the respiratory infection that she'd had for the past two weeks, the one that had sent them to the pediatrician in the first place.

"What does one look like?" The surgeon asked and looked at Nate. When Nate shook his head, the doctor sighed and held out his hand and curled his thumb and index finger into a small circle. "It's this big around, and about half an inch thick."

He'd already explained that they'd put it on her abdomen, and when she grew older they'd eventually move it up near her shoulder.

"You'll be able to feel it, of course," he said. "But it's a pretty complicated little piece of equipment. Costs more than my first car," he said. He paused and leaned against the frame of the door.

"Anything else?"

"Her chest congestion?" Stella asked.

"Stella," Nate said. "The anesthesiologist already went over that with us."

"Everything's ready," the surgeon coaxed. Nate then stood and shook the surgeon's hand and thanked him, a trusting smile playing with the edges of his mouth. Stella looked away from the two men and instead watched Gracie as she started to cry, her cheeks turning red from the strain. Gracie tried to tug at the wiring of her heart monitor, then gave up and reached again for her rattle.

When the Meditating Mother returned, she held a hot water bottle in one hand and a cup of coffee in the other. Her shirt was buttoned now, the collar raised on one side as if she'd put herself together in a rush. The hot water bottle was mauve pink rubber and bloated and looked like the old-fashioned kind Stella's mother used to put under the covers of her bed to keep her warm when she was growing up. The Mother handed Stella the cup of coffee—which turned out to be lukewarm tea—then she opened her palm and produced two pills.

"Take these," the Mother said. "For the fever and swelling."

Stella took the pills without asking what they were and then washed them down with the tea, which was sweetened with honey and soothed Stella's dry throat. Then the Mother leaned over Stella's breast and pressed the water bottle against her chest and held it there, her palm flat against the bottle to steady the wobbliness of the rubber. The warmth spread quickly and the pain eased away for the first time in three days.

"No cabbage leaves," the Mother said. "But they offered me lettuce." She smiled and put Stella's hand where hers was and then stepped back and sat again on the loveseat across from Stella.

"Thank you," Stella said.

The Mother looked at the ounce of milk Stella had been able to produce from the one breast. Stella held the bag in her lap protectively, and then the Mother glanced at the pile of empty plastic sacks with the other babies' names on them that sat stacked on the table next to the loveseat. "Most of these are gone. You'd think they'd understand how that might make us feel when we come in here. Having to see the names of all these babies," she said. She looked at the machine in the corner, now quiet. The Mother leaned back and stretched her arms over her head and yawned. "The nurses won't even look at me," she said. "That tells you all you need to know."

Stella felt the bottle cooling a little and she moved it to the other breast, which didn't ache as badly.

"No, keep it against the one that's infected," the Mother said. "It'll help bring the milk down."

It felt good to have someone who seemed to know what she was doing taking control and Stella did as the Mother said. The straps of Stella's nursing bra rested against her stomach, which bunched up over the wide band of her maternity jeans. In the harsh lighting, her stomach looked luminescent, a bright moon in the small room. In the days they'd been in the ICU, Stella had picked up on the rules of the parents: no questions, no open crying, no eye contact.

"He's not ours, really," the Mother finally said. "The baby, I mean. He's adopted. I've been taking these pills that are supposed to make me lactate, but so far nothing. Keep trying, they tell me. It'll happen, they tell me."

The machine stood silently next to Stella as if waiting, and she moved the hot water bottle away from her chest. Stella's breast had swollen larger than she imagined it could, and the pain made her eyes water. She thought of the Mother's baby boy in his crib, the tubes coming from his nose and mouth, and the small legs that the Meditating Mother massaged each morning for what seemed like forever.

The Mother got up and repositioned the water bottle and peeked underneath. "That has to feel better," she said, and Stella nodded. It occurred to her now why the Mother's baby's area, like Gracie's, was free from taped family photographs and cards. Stella hadn't wanted to put any up because somehow that would make Gracie's stay permanent. And maybe that's what the Mother thought, too. Or maybe she knew he would never move upstairs, or go home.

"We can try for another one, my husband says. I don't even know what he means when he says that." The woman's face was inches away from Stella's chest, the top of her bobbed hair interrupted by a white sliver of scalp. Finally, she gave up on positioning the hot water bottle and looked up at Stella. "What does that even mean?"

"I don't know," Stella said. She could feel the Mother's anger close around the two of them like the cuff of a blood pressure monitor, and Stella suddenly remembered the strange way Nate's face had turned bright red around his lips and eyes—like some sort of glowing raccoon—on the night before they brought Gracie in for her surgery and he had finally let himself cry.

"What does that even mean," the Mother said; it wasn't a question. Stella felt her face get hot and she sat the cooling water bottle flat against her thigh, her breast swollen and exposed. Stella kept her eyes on the Mother and didn't say anything. *One of the lucky ones*, she thought, and Stella imagined the Mother's boy—with his glowing white skin, his covered eyes, his list of medications—and she realized that she had never seen the baby move his head, or reach out to tug at the wires splayed across his chest.

"I'm sorry," Stella finally said.

The Mother pressed the palms of her hands against her lap, smoothing the creases that had formed in her linen pants. Then she pushed her hands through the wispy ends of her bobbed hair.

Stella waited for the Mother to answer, but instead, the woman turned her head and stared at the empty milk bags on the table in the corner next to her. After a minute, Stella saw the Mother move her lips, her voice almost a whisper as she began her chant. The names of the drugs had now become familiar to Stella, too, and she found herself reciting, almost prayer-like, along with the Mother as she reassembled the straps of her nursing bra, accidentally pinching the tender skin above her breast, and then pulled her shirt down to cover her stomach. Then Stella picked up the baggie of milk and walked past the Mother out of the room, her arm brushing against the Mother's on the way out.

Down the hall, Stella could see Nate talking to Dr. Tam, Gracie's still-full bottle in his hand, the plastic milk sacks on the chair behind him. *Captopril*, Stella whispered. *Digoxin*. Gracie's nurse, belly heavy against the side of Gracie's crib, reached to replace the IV bag that hung from the metal pole at the head of Gracie's crib. Dr. Tam said something to Nate and then paused, and Nate turned his head to look down the hall. Dr. Tam held a folder full of papers in his hands, charts of some sort, and he pointed at the top one but Nate looked at Stella instead.

Lasix, Potassium, Stella continued. *Upstairs. One of the lucky ones.*

Then she felt a rush of something warm and wet against her chest.

Breaking the Neighbors

The neighbor's cat is a whore under her house. Claire is in bed, sitting up, knees held to her chest in the sort of way she likes to hold them in movie theaters when she's bored. It's three in the morning and beneath her bed—coming from the crawl space underneath her house—there are low growls and moans that sound unusually loud tonight, like the groan the city's ancient tornado siren makes before it releases its piercing shrill. She believes she can smell the cats, too, their sour scent of urine and sperm all mixed up, a musty odor that comes through the wood and up to her mattress, into her flannel sheets. She climbs out of bed, finally, and kneels on the floor, head bent to the side and laid flat against the wood. She can hear them moving around down there, scratching their claws into the discarded trash under her house. She imagines the neighbors' orange cat—its fur matted with clumps of sewage and stale soil—with its back arched high, eyes closed, face covered with black like a bandit's mask.

The moans get louder until finally there's one last moan and the pornographic moment is over. Claire climbs back under the comforter and curls into her pillow. She buries her face and inhales the familiar stale, lemony scent of detergent. She's thinking of the neighbors next door, of Tammy and Nick, their long, thin legs pretzeled together as they sleep. She imagines their room, quiet and warm, the dog they call Hambone asleep at their feet. She reaches under the comforter to touch herself—thinking, first, of Nick's brown back, then Tammy's smooth stomach, the way the skin stretches tight over her ribs—but is too tired to bother. Underneath her, one of the cats hisses, and Claire closes her eyes tightly enough that she sees little white pinpricks of light, a fireworks display of frustration.

In the morning, Claire makes her way to the bathroom. Her arms are still sore from sleeping, her muscles are tense and her jaw aches from clenching. She has trouble with the joints and cartilage in her jaw, which the oral surgeon calls TMJ. The last time she went to see him he told her that he wanted to operate and crack the bone in four places. While he showed her X-rays and put the tips of his fingers over the white curve of her lower jaw, Claire thought about what they would use to crack the bone. A small hammer? Some sort of clamp? She thought about waking up with a mouth full of wire, her tongue rough and swollen from the rub of metal.

She runs water in the bathtub, testing the heat against her wrist. The sound of the water relaxes her and she closes her eyes and rests her back against the cool tile. In the living room, on the coffee table, is the stack of papers that came the day before from her husband's lawyer with the scheduled dates for their meetings. Instead of going in to work today, she imagines relaxing in the backyard hammock that has recently filled with dead leaves and twigs. The piles look like nests, small shelters for rabid animals. She could clean the hammock, though, and finally weed out the herb garden, poison the ant bed next to the night-blooming jasmine tree, bag the small hill of brush that has piled underneath the kitchen window. There is too much to do, too much that her husband has left for her, but she could at least start. She could skip work and buy a rake, a garden hose, a sprinkler that waves water back and forth in a fine, wide arc.

Her back tightens and she slips away from the tile and lowers herself into the heat of the bath, her body pulling away at first, then easing down into the warmth. Baths are new to Claire; she used to prefer the economy of showers. She stares up at the ceiling to avoid the white of her breasts, her thick thighs, too, spread and open. When she first married, she enjoyed the feel of her body. The size of her arms, her legs, felt solid. Her husband would step in behind her when she took a shower in the morning, saying, "I think I could get used to the feel of this body for the rest of my life, you know that?" Now she has the feeling that she's coming apart a little at a time. First, her jaw will go, and then her skin. It will peel away from her bones. The strips will come off in sections that she'll be able to stitch together and drape over the windows, to use as curtains.

Nick is on his front porch, watering his plants. His shirt is off and his vertebrae protrude somewhat obscenely, like a dinosaur skeleton in the Natural History Museum she saw once in Chicago. His ribs are like splayed fingers pushing up through tanned, smooth skin. He has his blond hair pulled back in a long ponytail. In Claire's yard, Hambone's pissing on one of the lilac bushes wedged up against her porch. She stomps on the wooden boards and the dog looks up with his weepy brown eyes, then resumes peeing. This is his favorite spot. The neighbor's animals are slowly taking over her house, marking her yard and the peeling grey planks of her house as their own.

Nick looks up and waves, then goes back to watering the plants, which are housed in huge buckets and have sizable leaves.

They are a beautiful green. Hibiscus, Claire thinks. In the afternoon sun, their big orange blossoms fall dead quickly and litter the neighbor's porch with brown scraps that are paper-thin. Tammy comes out of the front door and joins Nick. She's dressed in a red satin robe that ends at her knees and there are two dragons stitched on the back, coiled together as if locked in battle. She carries two cups of coffee across the wide expanse of the porch and waits with them until Nick looks up. Then she hands him one of the cups and sits on the step next to him, waiting as he tests the soil of the plant in the largest bucket. His hands, up to his wrists, covered with dark mud.

Nick has his own business cleaning cars. *Detailing*, he calls it. He's always making Claire feel guilty for running her car through the mechanical wash at the gas station, telling her she's killing the paint job each time she goes through. Parked in their driveway is a white van with *Nick's Auto Detailing* painted in black script letters along both sides. He hand-painted the lettering himself, and the words are slanted down, the last letters of *detailing* nearly merged together. Tammy works as a waitress in an upscale strip club where businessmen go for long lunches—a place with a buffet that stretches from one side of the room to the other and the sign out front boasts that it's the largest in the state. She only works three afternoons a week and makes more than Claire, who works full-time at the University Library. They moved into the house next to hers over six months ago, a week after her husband moved out, and Claire watched them for two months before they noticed her next door on the porch, only fifty feet away. The real estate agent who sold them the house told Claire that they'd paid practically nothing for the place because the foundation needed work. Still, the agent told her, even with the problems they lucked out. They could do a few minor repairs and turn around and sell it for an enormous profit, unlike Claire and her husband, who had bought too high and were now stuck with a loss. So far the only repair the neighbors have made is a cosmetic one—they painted the house a shocking white, even the shutters and front porch. The house glows at night, a bright tooth in the dark, dreary mouth of their street.

Besides Hambone and the orange tabby they call Irene, they also have a boa constrictor they keep in an aquarium in their laundry room. Sometimes Nick comes over with it draped over his shoulders. One time he gave Claire a skin the snake shed; she keeps it on the windowsill over her kitchen sink. The heat has made it brittle, like the shell of an insect cooked thin by the sun. Tammy stays inside most of the time when she's not at work. Claire will see her pass by their window, which is maybe twenty feet from her own living room window, above the couch. Tammy often wears a short tank top and cut-off jeans, her long arms pale and thin. All afternoon she goes back and forth, from the kitchen to the bedroom. Claire waits for Tammy to look across and see that she's being watched, inspected, but she never looks. Her head's always down or to the other side. Nick's skin is dark, his hair bleached from the sun. He rarely wears shirts. He looks good, but of course, they're both young—in their mid-twenties. Claire is a decade older than they are. They're like her younger cousins, the ones who come to family reunions with cases of beer and frisbees and who have to be driven home after drinking all day.

They're not like Claire and her husband were at their age, though. Claire's husband preached to her about the importance of 401k plans and necessary college accounts for future offspring, so Claire spent her Saturday mornings clipping coupons for their Sunday trip to the grocery store. These neighbors spend their money. Last week, Nick bought a new stereo system with digital surround sound and speakers five feet tall. Claire was on her front porch when two men in a brown van delivered the boxes, and she sat on the porch for over two hours and watched Nick, through the large window on the side of their house, opening the boxes. He ripped them open with his hands, throwing the papers and packing foam over his head like a child at Christmas. Nick listens to his music loud and sometimes plugs in his electric guitar and plays along with the music, which is always repetitive and heavy with bass. Sometimes he keeps the stereo going all night and Claire wonders how he has the energy to get up in the morning to spend the day wiping down cars.

Claire finishes her coffee and looks over at their front porch, now empty. Hambone lingers in her yard, then takes a slow step onto Claire's porch. When she doesn't move, he takes another. He dips his head and walks to where she's sitting, a trail of slobber wetting the boards behind him. When the front door slams at the neighbor's house, Hambone jumps over the side of Claire's porch and runs to Nick, his tail wagging like a frantic metronome. Nick crosses his own driveway, then Claire's yard, and Claire automatically pulls her terrycloth robe tighter across her chest.

When he comes up to the side of her porch and rests his arms on the wooden ledge, he glances down at her covered chest and smiles at her closed fist that bunches the front of her robe together. "You want to feed Irene while I'm out of town?" He smiles and looks over his shoulder, back at his house. "I'm just going camping. Tammy will be here, but the cat gets her upset."

"Why?"

"Cause she's in heat. I figure since she's always over here anyway, you could just put some food out."

Claire stares hard at Nick's shoulders, at the freckles that cloud the tops of them. He's scraping the calluses on the soles of his feet against the steps to her porch and the sound is dull and painful.

"Why don't you get her fixed?" Claire asks.

Nick looks up. "Why should I?" His eyes are red and watery and he narrows them before he looks away from Claire, out into the street.

"So she doesn't get pregnant."

"So what if she does?" Nick turns and smiles at Claire, flashing his teeth at her. "Cats get pregnant all the time."

Claire stands and she realizes that her left foot has fallen asleep. The pain makes her step back and she shakes her foot in quick, little motions. "I have to go to work." She takes a step towards the front door, but Nick puts his arm out and waves for her to stop.

"Look, Tammy has to take care of my plants. I'm afraid the cat's going to drive her crazy and she won't do anything right. The leaves look sick. Some sort of fungus."

"She can't water a few plants and put food in a bowl too?"

Nick crosses his arms and looks up at her, as if really considering Claire's question, then walks up onto the porch and over to the chair where Claire was sitting and pushes down on the back of it, flexing his muscles. His arms are long and thin, with little yellow hairs on the tops of his forearms. His chest is flat and brown and almost hairless, and the definition of the muscles makes Claire ache.

"How about this," he says. "I'll detail your car for you when I get back. Clean the interior and everything." He holds tight to the arm of the chair, his fingers white at the knuckles. "You can't get a cat fixed when it's in heat, anyway. They charge you for it. All that extra bleeding." He pushes too hard and the chair falls over and Claire jumps back a little at the noise. He smiles, then bends down to pick it up and Claire goes to her front door. She can feel the heat on her chest, rising.

"So you'll watch the cat, right?"

Claire doesn't turn to face him. Instead, she opens the front screen door and takes a step inside the house. "Leave the food in my mailbox," she tells him, then shuts the door behind her.

After she calls in sick, Claire sits on the couch in front of the television and starts to watch a soap opera. She has no idea who the characters are, but she likes the way someone is mentioned, and then the next scene starts with that character's face in close-up. Even though Claire never watches soap operas, and can't even puzzle together where this one is supposed to take place, she can still understand the storylines and put names to the faces on the screen.

She wastes time when she calls in fake-sick to work. She's always been plagued by the guilt involved, and so she often finds herself camped out on the couch when she does so, watching television. The guilt eats away at her stomach, erupts in her head like a giant balloon. It drove her husband crazy, the way she obsessed over small crimes until she was sick. She couldn't eat if there were dishes in the sink, or food spilled around the dog's bowl. She couldn't have sex until the floor was vacuumed. When they'd first met, she was hungry for the feel of her husband. She could have him all day and let the dirt pile up around them like a nest. But after they got married, they took each other on, and fought until things got labeled. His: den, second bedroom. Hers: kitchen and the bedroom they shared. Now he's not even fighting her for the house or the car. He wants nothing from her at all anymore.

Claire leaves the television on but reclines on the couch, closes her eyes to relax, and imagines a color. She learned this trick from one of the circulation librarians at work and has found that sometimes she can concentrate when she stops her thoughts and thinks only in shades and hues. She thinks blue, and sees a small bird with wings tucked neatly against its side, beak up in the air. She thinks yellow, and sees the same bird, in the same position, with yellow feathers the color of corn. When she thinks she will always see the bird she falls asleep, her arm trapped between her legs, her feet resting on the arm of the couch.

The phone wakes Claire up and her first thought is that someone has died. There was a hunger relief drive on the television when she woke briefly from her nap and it had her dreaming of gaunt children in dorm rooms, or what looked like dorm rooms, but how could that be? They were wandering naked in clusters, touching the walls.

Her jaw has an incredible ache and she has to open wide to pop it before she can speak.

"Hello? Claire?" The voice is girlish, almost a whisper.

"Yes, sorry. Who's this?"

"It's Tammy, from next door. Are you busy right now?"

Claire stretches her arms and pulls the phone cord tight until her tension lets go. "No," she says. "Just reading." Claire tries to remember if Tammy has ever called her before, or if she has ever called over to their house. She tries to remember if she gave them her number.

"Can I come over? I've got some beer."

Claire pauses, wondering what time it is, and Tammy says, "Claire?" Then, "Okay, I'll be right over," and hangs up the phone.

Claire wonders if she cleaned the bathroom recently, if she remembered to rinse the tub after her morning bath. She decides to make a quick check, but then she hears Tammy's footsteps on the stairs, amazed at how she crossed their two yards so quickly. Claire opens the door and Hambone is suddenly in her living room, circling mud on her hardwood floors. Tammy stands in front of the door, holding a six-pack of beer. She looks like she's twelve years old, a child without makeup, hair hanging limp over her shoulders.

"He follows me everywhere," Tammy says.

Claire stares at the paw prints the dog has tracked through her living room. The prints are everywhere, even under one of the chairs. Tammy walks into the room and puts the beer on the coffee table, then moves to the bookshelf in the corner of the room to look at the tiny glass sculptures Claire's kept since she was twelve.

"You find these at a garage sale?" Tammy picks up a giraffe by its neck and holds it to the light. The small glass animal is tiny and blue with green spots. The legs are delicate and brittle, impossible to repair. Claire feels her arms stiffen and she looks away, to the front door. She remembers opening the small box from her husband on her birthday the first year they were married and seeing the tiny giraffe, the only animal that wasn't given to her by her father.

"No," Claire finally says. She starts to say something about the dog, then stops herself. Instead, she shuts the door softly.

"Should I get some glasses?"

Tammy looks up, her long hair partially covering her eyes. "What for?" She shakes her hair, then puts the giraffe back in the wrong place, on the shelf with the picture frames. After that, she goes to the couch and sits down. She falls back, her arms stretched out to her sides and her legs spread open. Hambone follows her and curls up at her feet.

"Sit down," Tammy tells her. "Take a load off." She opens two beers and hands one to Claire, who rests it against her leg until Tammy says, "Have a drink, relax. God, you look like you're coming apart."

"I do?" Claire wonders just what coming apart looks like. Maybe the seams of her face have started to come unstitched, the bright bone underneath now glowing through the separation of skin.

Tammy lifts one leg, bends it, and rests her foot on the edge of the couch. "You do," she says, but instead of looking at Claire, Tammy glances around the room.

"Is anything wrong?" Claire finally asks her, and Tammy takes her eyes away from the front door to look at her.

"I can't sit still when Nick goes away. I hate being alone." She takes a long sip from her beer, then puts the bottle on the coffee table. "How do you *stand* it?"

Claire lets the question hang there and settles her eyes on the ring of water that has already formed on the table around the base of Tammy's beer. "I'm used to it," she says finally. Then, quietly, "I like it." When Tammy narrows her eyes, Claire feels the need to defend herself. "I used to be married," she says. She realizes this is the first time that she's spoken of her husband as an ex-husband and she's amazed at how easy it is to past-tense her marriage.

Tammy smiles and widens her eyes. "When?"

"I was eighteen when we got married."

"Where is he?"

"Gone," Claire says. "He was living here for a few days when you first moved in, I think." Then, automatically, she goes to the kitchen table, where the divorce papers are, and brings them to Tammy. "I got these yesterday," she says.

Tammy glances at the papers held in front of her and then sits back. "You got a picture? I don't remember seeing him." Tammy scratches her arm, stares at the dog, and Claire realizes that Tammy doesn't believe her. She wants proof, so Claire walks over to the bookshelf and slips out the hardback copy of *Leaves of Grass*. Inside, under the cover, she sees her ex-husband, his bad tux and uncomfortable smile, and herself, even younger than Tammy is now, in the high-necked lace dress that once belonged to her grandmother. She hasn't looked at the picture in years; it's the only one she's kept, and she's surprised at how young she looks, how smooth and full of hope. She carries the picture to Tammy, who holds the picture carefully, by the edges, as if it's contaminated.

"Not bad," she says. "He's got the full-on feathered hair thing going, doesn't he?" She hands the picture back to Claire, and she places it back into the book and closes the cover. "So what happened? He cheat on you?"

Claire thinks of the woman her husband has moved in with, her black curly hair and tanned legs. "No," she says. "We were just young. We grew up."

Tammy sips her beer and nods. "I don't think I'd leave Nick if he cheated. I mean, I'd be pissed and all, don't get me wrong. But marriage is supposed to be 'til death do us part, right? Like, in sickness, health, all that." She sips her beer and scratches at a rough patch of skin on her knee. "Also, I don't think I could live by myself. I keep telling Nick I want an alarm. The kind that calls the police. That way I won't have to keep getting up in the middle of the night to look out the windows. I keep thinking one of these nights there's going to really be someone there and then what would I do? Like, seriously?"

"Call the police?"

"Sure, but who knows what could happen. That would be the worst, to wake up and see someone right outside your window, looking in." She looks at Claire, then away. "But it's not like Nick's ever going to cheat anyway."

Claire watches Tammy bounce her leg up and down. She can't sit still. It exhausts Claire to watch her and it occurs to her that Tammy's on some sort of drug.

"You want to listen to some music? I've got some stuff next door. Really excellent mixes I made this afternoon. I'll be back in a sec." She walks out the door and Hambone follows her, his nails clacking against the wood of Claire's newly refinished floor.

Claire can't remember the last time she had sex. She can't look at Tammy without imagining her with Nick, alone, in bed. The two of them touching each other with an urgency Claire can barely remember. At night, when she imagines the two of them together, Claire sees Tammy as she takes Nick's fingers and leads them around her body like she's pointing out countries to invade on a map. Claire remembers sex with her husband, in the end, as a chore. If he bought her an appliance, a new blender, perhaps, or an iron, she'd feel obligated to him. Payment with her body, with her touch on his skin. But she never touched him, really, not in the end when things became so distant between them that they moved around each other and got good at pretending to care. After she got to know every curve of the muscles in his back, the length of his arms, she figured *what's the point*? Nothing erupted for them then. They kept each other silent. They did things in a methodical, half-hearted way.

Her ex-husband looked nothing like Nick when he was young, with his delicate fingers, like a girl's almost, and the smooth edges around the tips. The awkward, patchy beard he tried to grow after he quit grad school during his first year. He wanted to look older, get a job and move on with his life. He wanted kids, this house, a new car in the driveway. He was always frustrated and waiting for his life to begin and he started to blame Claire, but in a quiet way. He would sulk around the house, or stay on the couch in front of the television, telephone perched on the coffee table in front of him, as if waiting for someone to call and offer him the opportunity to finally be an adult. They would go whole days without speaking to each other sometimes. Then Claire got the job at the library—only part-time back then—shelving books, and she'd come home and find him in the backyard in the heat of summer, sitting in the grass in his sweat suit, reading car magazines, and she realized he had given up. Her husband, twenty-five, sunburned and silent, already disappointed with the way his life had turned out. He would look up at her sometimes when she would walk out to the backyard to bring him a glass of water and he would look confused, like he didn't recognize who she was. Then his eyes would drop to the ground and he'd frown, as if suddenly remembering. Even when he decided to go back to graduate school, where he would meet the woman with the dark curly hair, he would come home from classes quiet, shoulders pulled inward. He'd sulk his way up the front walk and Claire would fight the urge to bolt the door on him. They talked to each other at night in bed, politely, like strangers. After the first semester back, he started to change. He took her to dinner, to nighttime concerts in the park, and then he bought her blenders, toasters, an electric carving knife. He talked about kids again, but Claire felt disgusted. She was glad when he started to sleep with the woman. He walked out of the house with only a suitcase and a backpack full of his notebooks, his Chemistry texts, and his plastic bag of expensive mechanical pencils.

Tammy comes back without Hambone and Claire can hear him whining outside her door.
"I gave him something to chew on," she says. "He's a baby sometimes." She has a stack of compact discs piled against her chest and she looks around the room. "Where's the stereo?"
Claire stands and goes into her bedroom to get the portable radio/CD combo player she takes with her to work, to listen to the news when the weather's bad, or when there's a plane crash or a

court case she's interested in. She's not used to drinking alcohol, and her head feels heavy. Her mouth feels suddenly dry and she swallows twice. Tammy follows her back to the bedroom, still holding the discs. She looks at the small portable Claire unplugs and hands to her.

"No stereo?" Her voice is full of disappointment.

"I don't like music that much. I like it to be quiet."

"But maybe you'd like it if you had a good stereo. It just sounds better that way, without all the fuzz to mess things up."

Claire thinks about the giant brown boxes that sat in her driveway after Nick unpacked his speakers and how she had to break them down herself and carry them to the trash on pick-up day after he let them sit there for two days without moving them. "Maybe," Claire says. "You're probably right." She scratches her arm and stares at the tape player that Tammy holds against her leg. "I just don't think an expensive stereo is something I need."

Tammy starts to laugh, and Claire realizes that Tammy thinks she's joking—that she can't understand why anyone wouldn't want an expensive stereo with massive speakers. Tammy holds the small portable and inspects it, flips a few of the switches, then turns and Claire follows her back into the living room and watches her plug the player in and set it carefully on the coffee table, between two empty beer bottles. She sorts through the discs, inspecting the Sharpie scrawl that graffiti each silvery disc's face, and finally puts one in, adjusts the volume, then sits back. The song begins low and soft, not the heavy bass of the loud death metal Claire was expecting.

"Nick's gone because we've been fighting a lot lately. He says I do things to get to him. Like scratch his car, mess with his plants." Tammy stretches her arms out in front of her. "He says if I mess up anything else he'll know I'm doing things to get to him on purpose. It's crazy. Why would I want to make him mad?" She has the music on low and the song turns hard, the beat strong and fast. She twists her arms in front of her and Claire stares at the light stubble under her arms, at the crevice where her armpit caves in and a small scar cuts through the hairs. Tammy closes her eyes and taps her foot against the floor. The bass starts to thump. The methodical beat reminds Claire of the cats pounding under her house, of Hambone scratching at her door, into the wood.

"Is that how things started to go south with your husband? You do things to him to get him mad?" Tammy's voice is accusatory and Claire becomes defensive.

"It's not always the woman's fault, you know. Sometimes the man's the one with the problems."

Tammy smiles and looks away. "You want another beer?" she finally asks. Claire shakes her head no, and Tammy opens another beer and drinks it half down in one swallow, her eyes closed, one arm stretched now across the back of the sofa. "I dance to this song at work," she says, smiling.

"The waitresses have to dance, too?" Claire can't imagine the way Tammy would dance. She wants to see Tammy move her arms, her legs. She wants to see how she excites Nick when they're alone, at night, in the dark. In their house, while the cats are awake and Claire is, too.

Tammy opens her eyes. "No, the waitresses wear bikinis and serve drinks and don't make shit for tips. I was a waitress for a while, but a spot opened up and Nick talked me into it. I didn't think I could do it, all those old guys staring at my tits, but it's not so bad. I get good money."

"You don't feel bad about dancing naked for men?"

Tammy rolls her eyes and puffs her cheeks, a childish gesture. "You sound like my mother," she laughs. "Like my *grandmother*."

Claire thinks about the men and the wadded bills they must keep fisted in their laps until they feel confident enough to slip them shyly, like misbehaving schoolboys, under the thin strap of Tammy's g-string and the power she must feel when that happens, the control she has over those men when they slip her that money. Claire feels suddenly jealous, then ashamed. "Can you show me your dance?" She looks away when she asks this.

Tammy lifts one of her shoulders up and drops her head to one side. When she finally speaks, her voice sounds tired. "I don't have my *costume* or anything, but I'm pretty good. I get paid fifty bucks for a lap dance."

"You don't dance on a stage?"

"Well, yeah, but lap dances are where the big tips come from. They have rules, though, so nothing gets out of hand."

"What sort of rules?"

"Like no touching my breasts, no trying to kiss me. That sort of stuff."

"Does that happen a lot? People trying to touch you?"

"You wouldn't believe it. Some of them are real assholes." Tammy leans over and turns up the volume on the portable. "But sometimes it's fun. Some of them are nice." She stands up, then walks around the coffee table to the other side of the room. She faces away from Claire, stretches her arms over her head, and says, "Watch this opening, it's the best part. It took me two weeks to get it working right." She slips her tank top over her head and pushes her hair up. Her ribs are visible under her skin, which is white and almost pale blue in places. She collapses onto the floor, bent forward, and when the music starts up again, she goes slowly to her knees and turns to look at Claire. She has her finger in her mouth and looks to the side of Claire, not really seeing her, but concentrating her gaze on a spot on the wall behind Claire's head. Then Tammy moves her hips, her jean shorts still on, low. The pink cotton waistband of her underwear peeks out over the rim of her shorts. She straightens herself slowly and rubs her tiny breasts in an awkward motion, then puts her finger back in her mouth and sucks on it.

Claire turns her head away, embarrassed.

Tammy looks even younger like this, like a child doing an obscene version of her spring dance recital routine to scare her mother. She concentrates on the wall, her fingers moving in perfect little circles across her skin, and Claire wonders if this is the dance she does for Nick, if this is what she excites him with, these cardboard movements and choreographed suckings.

Claire's husband was easy to excite, too, in the beginning. She remembers the way she'd take off her nightgown for him, the way she'd practice during the day, in front of a mirror, to get the tilt of her head right, the position of her arms.

Claire can feel her heartbeat in her throat. Her head pounds and she feels the pain in her jaw, a throbbing that makes her teeth ache. She wants to go to Tammy and grab her arms, hold them behind her back until the dancing stops and the bass beat clears from her head. She suddenly wants to break one of Tammy's delicate wrists, wants to twist her arm hard enough to hear the bone snap underneath her grip.

"Can you talk to me?" Tammy's eyes close and her mouth opens a little.

"What?"

Tammy opens her eyes and looks at Claire, frustrated. She reaches over and pushes the pause button on the portable. "The men talk to me when I dance." She starts the music again and closes her eyes. "Say something," she says. "Tell me how hot I am. You know, sexy stuff." She rubs her hands between her legs and tosses her head back. "Tell me how I make you feel."

Claire thinks she can imagine the exact look on Tammy's face when the bones in her wrist snap, the look in her eyes when she realizes that Claire will not stop until she feels the break. "You're beautiful," Claire says, and understands that what she feels is hate, the same hate she felt for her husband before he left. Tammy is a disappointment really, a spoiled child. Was Claire like that once? In the wedding picture, in her grandmother's dress, did she think she deserved whatever she asked for?

Tammy's eyes are still closed; she doesn't break routine. When the music stops, she bows, then picks her tank top off the floor and slips it back over her head. She claps for herself, clearly pleased. The song shifts to something low and quiet and Claire stands, her legs weak.

Tammy walks to the couch to help Claire stand. "Too much to drink? Man, you're a lightweight." She wraps her fingers around Claire's arm gently, like a mother, and Claire pulls away. But Tammy moves close to Claire again, arms held out, and smiles. "Hey, what's the matter? Is it those stupid papers?"

Claire feels herself getting upset, like she's about to start crying, and she looks over at the divorce papers, which are spread out on the coffee table. Tammy has used the top page as a beer coaster and wet rings litter the page, smearing the black ink. When she speaks, she's surprised by how loud her voice is. "Do you think this is easy? Something stupid?"

Tammy starts to say something, then stops. She has her hand, which is cold and a little wet from the beer bottle, on Claire's upper arm. She holds her hand there, then picks up the remaining two beers from the table and holds them close to her chest, protectively, before she walks to the door. When Tammy turns around to look at Claire she looks like a child again, a twelve-year-old girl. Her eyes are dark and mean. "You won't forget to feed Irene, will you?"

Claire is confused, then she remembers the box of cat food Nick left in her mailbox.

Tammy turns back to the door when Claire doesn't answer. "She gets hungry at night and Nick said you promised." She stands in front of the door, her shoulders back, then turns and looks Claire in the eyes.

"Sure," Claire says, and Tammy's face softens, her eyes go down to the floor, and she smiles. She hugs the beers to her chest and they rattle. When she turns and walks out the door, Claire can see her shoulder blades held back and pointing through the thin cotton of her shirt and they look like the wings of a delicate bird. She stops on the porch and turns to Claire, her head still down, eyes on the floor. "See you later, okay?"

Claire stands on the porch and listens to the low slap of Tammy's feet on the sidewalk until they hit the grass at the edge of the yard and disappear.

In the night, a thunderstorm moves in and Claire wraps the comforter around her shoulders and goes outside to look at the rain under the street lamp in front of her house. When the rain starts to come in hard sheets, a wind kicks up and the streets begin to flood and the smell of the yard is fresh and green. She stands on the porch, in her underwear, with the yellow comforter damp around her. Tammy's and Nick's house, the fresh white of it, is slick and beautiful and Claire steps down, in the rain, and the ground is soft under her feet. She sinks into the mud when she walks across her lawn.

Next door, the neighbors' house is quiet. The window to Tammy's bedroom is a dark bruise on the bright face of the house. Claire stops in the middle of her gravel driveway to bend and wipe her feet, which are heavy with mud. She leans against the side of her car for balance and is surprised to see the red can of gasoline Nick uses to fill his lawnmower next to one of the tires. She looks across her driveway and littered around her front yard is Nick's tool chest, the blue tarp he uses to cover his van, a shiny silver hubcap. Claire feels an unexpected anger and the feeling settles in her chest, a hard, tough knot she imagines spreading, gradually, until her entire body is taken over by it.

She lifts the gas can carefully, with one hand underneath the bottom to keep it steady, and carries it to the neighbors' porch, to the row of plants on the edge of the stairs. In the rain, the dark leaves shine, wide and exotic. Her comforter sags on her shoulders and she drops it on the ground next to the neighbor's porch and stands in front of their house, almost naked. She unscrews the rusted top to the gasoline and bends over the plant closest to her on the porch. She puts her hand deep in the soil and feels for the roots, which are delicate and numerous, like veins. They tug out easily. She pours the gasoline into the gap in the soil. The smell is sharp, making her gag a little as she goes to each plant and soaks the roots. When the can is empty, she throws the metal container into the neighbor's front yard. It lands beside the small magnolia tree next to the cracked, wide sidewalk by the street.

When she steps down from the porch and walks back to her driveway, a brief excitement settles over her, then a calm she hasn't felt for years. She bends over and drags the tarp, heavy with rain, across the neighbor's yard and leaves it draped over the railing of their front porch. Then Nick's tool chest gets carried over and left in a puddle of water that has pooled up against the side of the neighbor's house, next to their cracked foundation. The hubcap gets thrown and settles next to the empty gas can.

When she's finished, she stops next to her car and turns to look back to the neighbors' house. In the newly-lit window of the bedroom, Claire sees Tammy's shape, the outline of her body, and she lets her arms fall to her sides and she leans back against the wet coolness of her car. She waits for the shape to move, but Tammy remains still, and Claire can almost see her face, the small eyes, looking out at her. Claire lifts her right arm and holds her hand up to shield her eyes from the falling rain, but the shape moves away, slips off to the side, and Claire steps away from the car and goes back home.

Small Bursts of Kindness

If this were a story, I'd give this guy a history. An interesting past, complete with a child, a son—who would be left an orphan—and also a disease. Maybe cancer, a rotten blackness in his lungs, spreading. He'd have a month to live, perhaps, anyway. So he'd have good reason to kill himself and we'd be able to explain to ourselves why he did what he did. We could all sit down, at one of the meetings the General Manager holds in the Eleventh Frame Lounge on a weekday morning when the place is empty, and lean back in the chairs even though we've been told this ruins the carpets, and we'd chain smoke while Pat, the GM, explained to us the details of the cancer, the reason why this pinsetter, this man with long black hair who seemed, for all we knew, to live out of the small room at the back of the bowling alley, why this man at some point between two A.M. and six A.M. on Saturday night, just three nights ago, in fact, hanged himself from the large oak tree out back next to the dumpster.

And we'd have known about his one-bedroom apartment in the section 8 housing complex on the west side of town, the *wrong* side of town, where the Mexican kids wander the streets next to the railroad tracks in loose gangs, looking for walls to tag with their own spidery language. We would have all been over there at some point or another, for a party on a Friday night, after the alley closed down and we were all a little too wired to go home to our kids, our own bad apartments. We'd be able to describe the stained plaid couch shoved up against the front window, the bathroom with cat hair pooled in the corners, the faded flowered paper covering only one wall in the kitchen. We'd be able to tell this man here in front of us, this cop in brown polyester who we all know from his moonlighting work here at the alley, this guy we don't even consider a real cop, just a fat guy with doughy skin who walks the lanes on Saturday nights busting underage drinkers, we'd be able to tell this guy about the pinsetter named Bill. We'd be able to give all the reasons why this guy walked out back, drunk, but sober enough to slip knot a rope, form a noose, and then climb up on top of the dumpster and sort of jump and swing himself away and hang himself from that tree.

I'd probably give him a more interesting name, too. One with a little drama. Something tragic. Dante, Absalom, or maybe just Shelby (because this is Texas, a state where mothers prefer to name their sons with a slightly effeminate touch, maybe to counteract any future violence, or maybe to get them beaten up early on, so they'll be tougher later in life). But I wouldn't choose Bill, which seems so generic, so uninteresting. Bill is a name for an unimaginative child's pet, a bird or a cat.

The truth is we *are* all sitting in the bar at one of those meetings, all twenty-two of us hourly-wage workers, and a wall of smoke settles just over us, over our heads, and Pat is explaining the reason we've all had to drag ourselves in here this morning (which he thanks us for) and why Reg the cop is standing behind him, with his pad of paper out, and pen, and his brown polyester shirt tucked neatly into his pants, which isn't how we usually see him on Saturday nights. And we all stare at our ashtrays, or the table tops, and sip flat Coke through plastic straws between drags on our cigarettes. Pat has his hands folded in front of him, and he's dressed in a dark blue suit and a striped tie with a bowling pin tack (a present from the previous GM) and looking official as he explains to us what we already know. The story was already written up in the local paper on Sunday, complete with pictures of the tree behind the alley, and everyone spent Sunday on the phone, playing tag with the workers they knew because the alley was closed for the day and so no one had to work, even though there were three birthday parties scheduled. The workers spent the day on the phone, spreading rumors about drugs, how one of the other pinsetters had heard that Bill owed a bunch of cash to some Mexican kids for pot, though no one had ever seen him smoke, or smelled anything on him. By the time I was called the drug had become cocaine and the people he owed money to were Russian graduate students at the University. (Why Russian? Whose fabrication was that? My guess was Cindy, the snack bar worker with a dramatic flair).

Then Pat introduces Reg, which is pointless, because, as I've told you, we already know who this guy is. Reg steps forward, adjusts his glasses, and thanks Pat, who backs away and takes a seat at one of the stools at the bar. There's a big inflatable blimp over his head, a promotional toy from Miller Lite celebrating the upcoming Super Bowl, and Pat glances up at it while Reg clears his throat, and then he, too, thanks us for coming out so early in the morning, although it's ten A.M., not so incredibly early. In fact, there are inflatable toys hung up all over the place in this room, plastic things in shapes of beer bottles, margarita glasses, footballs. Hung up to cover the predictable western theme of the room, the gaudy stagecoach wheel chandeliers, the horseshoes and glued lassos on the walls. In fact, right now, over the table in the back corner of the room under the dartboard, where the other pinsetters are all sitting, is a giant Jose Cuervo bottle and one of the teenage boys (all the pinsetters are teenagers, which is why they're all going to say they didn't know Bill, who was the old guy, in his forties, although he did buy the angry teenage pinsetters their kegs for their parties, in exchange for twenty bucks) pokes at the bottom of the bottle with his finger, his arm stretched up over his head, and only stops when Reg looks back at him and frowns, and the rest of us turn to stare at him, too.

"We're just trying to get information," Reg says, not very official sounding (he has an unusually high voice, and he stutters), but he's giving it his best shot, we can all tell. "So I'm here to see what you all remember from Saturday night. If Bill said anything, if you remember him drinking..." (here everyone turns to me—the bartender on duty Saturday night) "or if he had a fight with anyone, or said something..." (a pause—two s-words in a row always sets Reg's stutter off) " S-suspicious?" Reg looks at us hopefully, as if we're his children, and he puts his pen to the pad of paper, waiting. We all want to please him, at least I do, but I'm unwilling to admit that I had this deal with Bill, though I didn't really know him and can't remember how this agreement started, where I'd give him free tap beer during his breaks and he'd slip five bucks into my tip jar at the end of the night. Of course, I'm not willing to say that here, in front of the GM, for obvious reasons. And what would that information offer, anyway? He'd only had one free beer on Saturday night, as far as I can remember.

We all turn back to the table with the pinsetters. There are four of them now, without Bill, and three of them are leaning back in their chairs, smirking, their faces pink with fresh explosions of acne. They could not care less about the carpets. Then there's the fourth one, Philip, who is kind, and sweet, and is the one all of us ladies at the alley take care of because we feel sorry for him. He gets picked on by the others, because he's fat, and his Mom left his Dad last year to move in with one of the women on her bowling team, and those two women kiss during league play, and hold hands in the bar, and they even got tattoos on their arms with each other's names inside hearts, and so he gets especially picked on by the other pinsetters, who call him "queer" and "faggot" and make him oil down the lanes every night, regardless of the assignment sheets, and so we all go out of our way to show him attention, and feed him free food from the snack bar, and sometimes show up to cheer him on during county junior league tournaments.

All of us turn to those guys, waiting, since they seem to be the obvious source of information, but the kids all smirk at Reg, except Philip, who opens his mouth, about to speak, until one of the other teenagers hits him in the arm and Philip closes his mouth and winces. Reg, being the observant cop, notices this and calls Philip's name.

"You got something to say, Son?" Reg asks (he calls all the boys "son" and all the girls "darlin'," which is so Texas, so stereotypically southern, that I should probably leave this out.)

Philip looks at Reg and shakes his head, but Reg, being the cop that he is, won't let Philip off so easily. "You got something to say, boy, by God, you better speak up." And maybe it's the "by God," added for emphasis, that makes Philip feel guilty, and so he ignores the hisses from the other pinsetters and spills out a story about Bill buying them a bottle of Jack Daniels on Saturday afternoon and how the whole bunch of them sat in the back and drank shots while the bowlathon was going on. The kids drank and watched Bill work on a malfunctioning ball return on lane twenty-one.

"You boys were drinking back there? On the clock?" Pat stands up from his bar stool and his cheeks are red now, his forehead wet with sweat and oil. He's angry, not so much by the drinking, which is bad, but because they got away with it. Pat, as the GM, should know how to fix a set machine, and a ball return, but he rarely steps foot back behind the lanes. Those kids could have a party back there every night, complete with strobe lights and strippers, and Pat would never know. He was back there his first week on the job, saw a few rats, and hasn't been back there since.

Philip scratches at the table with his fingernail and the other pinsetters kick at his legs under the table.

"Ow," Philip looks up at the boy across from him. He looks hurt, upset, and all the women at my table coo and snicker.

"Well, there's a start," Reg says. "What else?" Reg writes in his pad like a fourth-grader, his tongue stuck out to the side, between his lips, and his fingers gripping the pencil too tightly. Pat starts to say something else to the pinsetters about their drinking but Reg shoots him a look and Pat sits back down on the barstool. He keeps his eyes on the table of pinsetters, though, and raises his eyebrows at the boys. The boys are poking at the inflatable toys again, and still kicking at Philip, who is now trying to hold back tears.

"What else?" Reg asks, and Philip looks up from the table and shakes his head.

"Nothing else," he says. "We drank a bit, then the bowlathon got done and Bill told us to go oil the lanes. When I clocked out, he was still back there." Philip pauses, then looks my way. "I didn't have but two or three drinks," he says. "Small ones." I smile at him, to show him I know he's still a good boy, still my favorite, still welcome to come in and shoot a game of pool with me at the end of his shift. I have a couple of slug quarters I've put on a string and I use that to get us free games of pool at the table, a trick Gerald, my sometimes boyfriend, taught me. I also use a flat spreader knife to jimmy the dollar slot on the jukebox to play music for free, Tom Petty's *American Girl*, which is a song Philip and I play at least ten times a night.

Somehow the other pinsetters get away with answering stupid *yes* or *no* questions, which we all think don't really have anything to do with Bill, or why he killed himself, but are probably just Reg's way of getting the surly boys to speak. The boys answer "Yessir" and "Nossir" to these questions and then we're all allowed to leave except for Philip, who Reg thinks knows more than he's telling. Everyone gets up and then groups themselves outside the swinging doors to the bar while Philip is forced to stay in the Eleventh Frame Lounge with Reg and Pat. I hang around, too, just to make sure he's okay. I sit at the table and watch Philip shuffle up to Pat and Reg, his tennis shoes moving against the carpet in slow scratches, his fingers running across the green felt of the pool table as he works his way around it and over to the barstools where Reg and Pat wait. No one seems to notice me until Philip glances over his shoulder at me, smiles, and rolls his eyes. This gets to Pat, this eye roll, and he stares back at me.

"Is there a reason you're not out of here?" he asks me and I stand. My right foot has fallen asleep and it tingles when I start to walk. I balance my weight on my left foot and sort of hobble over to where the three of them are standing. When I get to them they all look at me, waiting. I'm an outsider at this place, because I only bartend part-time, to supplement the income I get from working the Physics lab at the University where I set up ballistic pendulums and dub weekly exam tapes for undergrads. I didn't major in Physics, but the job seemed interesting enough to me two years ago when I graduated and I've grown comfortable with it. I majored in film, though, and so I applied a few weeks ago for an editing job in Dallas working on a kid's show about a dog who assumes the roles of different famous literary characters. I'm still waiting.

Most of the other workers are full-time and have worked at this bowling alley for years. They don't trust me, especially Pat, who only finished a year of community college before he was offered an assistant manager position at a Brunswick Alley in Fort Worth before they transferred him here, to Denton, almost a year ago. I don't talk about my other life at the University here, though. Instead, I waste time on my shifts gossiping with the snack bar workers about cheating husbands and family vacation disasters. And protecting Phillip, whom I have known for three years now, and who is seventeen and in high school. I give him fake-passionate kisses on his cheeks in front of the other pinsetters, who seem smitten with my large breasts and blond hair. I know how to get to those boys because I knew boys like them in high school and in college. I know those boys will grow up to be angry frat kids—the kind of boys who will worry about hazing paddles and cheap beer hangovers. They'll worry about not sleeping with enough girls. I know that kissing Philip in front of them makes them crazy because I'm older and experienced, but not too old to be over the hill. I'm still in the game, a girl who flirts for tips from the horny rednecks who flock to the bar to escape their wives and girlfriends, the women who yell at them when they gutter out on the tenth frame.

Now I put my hand on Philip's shoulder and squeeze, and he rests his head on my shoulder and I can feel the sweat soak through my varsity bowl T-shirt. He sighs and I feel the bulk of his stomach press against me and I brush his hair out of his eyes. Pat and Reg watch us closely, suspiciously, and I look behind them at the row of liquor bottles lined up against the back wall. From here I can see the small army of gnats that have invaded the liquor shelves and which are concentrated around the red plastic tips of the pour spouts of the amaretto and tequila bottles.

"I'm tired," Philip says. Pat and Reg look at Philip, then me, and I feel like I should say something to defend Philip, who is just a kid, an innocent teenager, and who has been through too much as it is. I wonder where his mother is right now, and why she's not here.

"Shouldn't someone call his mother?" I ask. "Doesn't she need to be here if you're going to ask him questions?" I feel like the outcast again, the girl with too much education for her own good.

"No one's accusing him of anything," Reg says. "I'm just trying to get some facts down about what went on here Saturday night. Philip's a good kid. He knows to do the right thing here." Reg still holds his pad of paper, and from where I'm standing I can see two words written on the piece of paper (Jack Daniels) in large, bubbly cursive.

"I don't want to get fired," Philip says. "It wasn't my fault about the liquor." He lifts his head from my shoulder but keeps his hand on my arm. He looks scared, and upset, and still like he's about to cry.

"No one's getting fired," Pat says. "I won't lie to you, though. I'm disappointed in you. You should know better than to be drinking, especially on a Saturday night. What if one of the lanes had gone down? What if I needed you?" Pat fingers the pin on his tie and then crosses his arms over his chest. "No one's getting fired here."

"Well good," Reg says. "Now, why don't you tell me about what Bill did that night? What did he say to you boys?"

"Nothing," Philip says. His voice goes high and he finally starts to cry. "It's just like I said. We gave him five bucks each and he went down to the store and got us a bottle and that's it. I think he had, like, one drink from it. Then he worked by himself on lane twenty-one. He didn't say nothing to us."

I stand with Philip while Reg makes him tell the whole story again and I think about the cleaning I will have to do later that night, how I will have to wipe down all the bottles, and the shelves, and then will have to leave Pat another note to call the exterminators again. I should run the blender through the dishwasher, too, since I have only been hand-rinsing it for the past week and there's probably gunk built up under the blades. I'll have to order more Budweiser, at least four cases, and then more margarita mix since Saturday night's special wiped us out.

"Can you take me home?" Philip asks. His face looks a little swollen and his eyes are now red.

"Of course," I say.

Reg looks defeated, and frustrated, and I know he expected more drama than he's getting. On slow Saturday nights, he sits in the bar with me and tells me stories about drug raids he's been on, and about flying over the fields in Krum, looking for a rumored acre of marijuana plants. I don't believe these stories, of course, but I listen and let Reg puff his chest. I imagine he spends most of his time busting up parties around the campus and he probably has been waiting a long time for something like this to happen at the bowling alley, which he's always seen as his turf, his property to protect.

I look at Reg's pad of paper before we leave and I see that he's underlined "Jack Daniels" twice, but has written nothing new. I walk Philip out through the beer cooler, then behind the snack bar and out the side door of the alley. I don't want the pinsetters to see that he's been crying. I know they're waiting for him. Waiting to pummel his faggoty ass into the ground for opening his big fat mouth.

Cindy the snack bar worker cares for Philip, too. Except she makes sexual innuendos and sometimes even kisses him on the mouth, even though she's almost twice his age. She is feeding chicken strips to Philip at a booth across from the bar window when I come in later that night to set up my stations. She is *feeding him chicken strips*. She is sticking out her pinky finger and dipping the strips in a small pot of barbecue sauce and then holding them up for him to bite.

Inside the bar, there is a table of dayshift workers sharing a pitcher of Coke and talking about Bill. I listen to them as I chop limes, pull cherries out of a jar taller than my forearm, and scrub the blender with a wire brush. Someone has heard that Bill sold drugs behind the alley, or maybe that's where he did drugs. Every story involves drugs and money, and I wonder where these people are getting these ideas. Television? Movies? At least one of them should have fabricated a bitter ex-wife by now, or a jealous lover. Someone should have developed a theory of murder.

I sort through the cooler and count bottles of Budweiser, Shiner, and Miller Genuine Draft. I try to remember which beer is popular with the Monday leaguers.

"You hear about his kid?"

I look up and one of the daytime snack bar workers, a woman who is usually gone as soon as her shift is over, is leaning over the bar, grabbing for the cherries I have just spooned out. She pops one in her mouth, satisfied with her bit of information.

I take her bait. "What kid?" She leans closer and I push the cherries closer to her, my payment for her bit of gossip.

"He had a kid with a woman over in Lewisville. A boy. Reg went and talked to the kid's mother this afternoon."

"How do you know?" Through the window to the side of me, I can see Philip, now sitting alone, staring out over the lanes.

"Reg called Pat and told him this afternoon. Someone working the front desk overheard him on the phone." The woman, still in her bright red snack bar vest, leans back and smiles. She takes a few more cherries and walks away slowly, back to the table of workers in the corner. I know this rumor is false because Pat's office is way in the back corner of the building, too far from the front desk to overhear a phone conversation. And besides, why would Reg keep Pat updated?

The table of workers stays past the first round of league play, past eight, and I refill their pitchers of Coke for free, from the bar gun that sometimes mixes soda water with the Coke and produces a watered-down product most customers complain about. I admire the mountain of cigarette butts the group produces but not the rest of their trash (candy wrappers, empty cigarette packs, napkins), which I will have to sweep up after they leave. After the bit of gossip about the kid in Lewisville, the only interesting piece of news I catch is about Philip, who supposedly found a suicide note taped to the wall behind lane sixteen a few hours before closing on Saturday night. One of the desk workers wants to get into Philip's locker in the back, where he keeps his spare bowling shoes and some towels, a resin bag. Supposedly the note is in there. I doubt this story, too, because I know that Philip wouldn't have a reason to keep the note. Besides, lane sixteen is where they set up the kids' bumper lane on Saturdays and Bill never worked that end of the alley.

On breaks, other workers stream into the bar for gossip updates. And the workers aren't the only ones interested. Leaguers, the ones who normally order their drinks at the pick-up window, actually come into the bar and sit down. They ask about news as if Bill were a close friend of all of ours, someone they knew well. They ask questions delicately, shaking their heads. One woman, a middle-aged league regular who also comes to the bowlathons on Saturday nights, even suggests she was having an affair with Bill. I try to imagine this woman with her frizzy perm and cat-appliquéd sweatshirts in bed with Bill, a man who wore Harley Davidson T-shirts and who refused to cut his hair, even when Pat threatened to fire him because his long hair was a potential danger (could get caught in one of the ball returns) and I just can't. Still, I smile at her suggestion and offer her free cherries, too, which she takes and pops in her mouth whole, stem and all. I realize that this is the first night in my three years of working at the alley that I have talked to this many people. Usually I stick to my regulars, some of the snack bar workers, and Philip. Then I realize that the bar is filled with women. All women. This never happens. Usually, the Eleventh Frame Lounge belongs to the men, the room in the alley where the worn-out wives send the birthday strippers they hire for their husbands. There is nearly one "exotic dancer" a week now, a regular happening, and so the women have taken over the booths across from the snack bar. I watch over the women dutifully, fully expecting the men to come in and reclaim their territory, but the men never come. The women pack the tables until eleven, when they stream out into the parking lot in clusters of threes and fours, leaving behind their husbands.

Philip doesn't come see me until midnight, when he sneaks in through the beer cooler while I'm cleaning up. Gerald, my sometimes boyfriend from the Physics Lab, a grad student who helps me dub the lab experiment tapes, is sitting at the bar, drinking a beer and waiting for me to clean up. He shows up here when he's bored, to drink for free, and we always wind up sleeping together, or coming close to. Tonight I've been telling him about Bill and he keeps changing the subject. He doesn't understand the excitement and I can't explain it to him because I don't either. I tell him that maybe I can't keep from talking about Bill because I've never known anyone who's killed themselves. I've never even known anyone who has died, except for my grandmother when I was ten years old. But tonight I've heard a hundred stories about suicides in cars, in homes, in garages, on public transportation. One leaguer even broke down crying when she told a story about a man she watched jump to his death from a bridge over the Red River.

Philip ignores Gerald and walks right up behind me. "Stay and bowl a game?" he asks, a sort of demand rather than a question. He doesn't look me in the eye; instead, he stares past me, into the mirror that lines the wall behind the liquor bottles. He doesn't shift his feet, or lean away from Gerald as he usually does.

"Can't," I say. I rub my hand over his mess of hair and then push past him to pull out the top shelf from the dishwasher. I let the steam from the hot glasses wash over my face. I can feel Philip behind me, the bulk of him, and I wait for him to move, or say something, but he just stands there. To the side of me, I can see Gerald, amused, about to make a crack about Philip's fat stomach.

"Something the matter?" I turn around and ask Philip.

"Everything's fine," he finally says. He avoids looking at Gerald and instead twists the plastic cap of the blender around and around until it pops off in his hand and he drops it into the sink. He finally leaves and I can hear him go back through the beer cooler and slam the door.

After Philip leaves, Gerald pushes his empty beer glass across the counter to me and stands. "You shouldn't encourage Fatty," he says. Then, when I begin to rinse the line of glasses in front of me, crusty with beer foam, he asks if I've heard from the dog people yet. He is the only person I've told about my job interview in Dallas and I regret that I chose him. He's made jokes about the show ever since. He doesn't realize that interview is the first thing I've taken seriously since I graduated. I don't care if it is a job editing dog-in-costume footage. I want it. It's a way out of the comfortable rut I've made for myself.

"So my place or yours?" I joke. I close the dishwasher and flip the switch and the noise fills the space between us. Gerald leans across the bar and kisses me too hard, his teeth accidentally biting my lower lip.

Bill is everywhere. We see him more than when he was alive—on lane twenty-one, his favorite lane (which is now the one a group of women is trying to convince Pat to commemorate with a plaque), in the jalapeño poppers at the snack bar (where someone has taped "Bill's Favorite!" next to the price on the menu), in the face of the new kid Pat hired to take Bill's place (doesn't he look just like a young Bill?). We talk about him, too. Over the next two weeks, three other leaguers and two front desk workers will also claim to have had an affair with Bill. He's become a lover, a passionate one, who, with one woman or another, had sex in the ladies' bathroom, on the front check-in desk, in the parking lot in a red Camaro, and on the couch in Pat's office. In one week, he's gone from a drug pusher to a sexed-up saint for the downtrodden bowlers' wives.

I've grown used to the women in the bar, their cheap perfume mixing with the scent of their cigarettes and strawberry margaritas. They've started dressing up for league play, as if they're competing with each other for some prize; some of the hairstyles are the most elaborate I've ever seen, complete with twisted braids and spiked bangs, white streaks and corkscrew tendrils. What one of them will eventually win I can't figure out. They wear their best and tightest black jeans, in mourning, and their black western shirts unbuttoned enough to reveal black lace bras. I have started referring to them as "Bill's girls," (for example, a man will ask: "Have you seen my wife?" and I'll answer "Bill's girls are in the bar, back corner." Not surprisingly, the men don't laugh. Instead, they stiff me on my tip).

The men come to the window to get their drinks and flirt and I serve them pitchers of Bud Light and smile, still thinking about the fractals Gerald has started to leave for me on my computer at work when we're slow—beautiful repeated patterns of color he makes from mathematical equations. I'm not sure where these small bursts of kindness are coming from, but I suspect they're sympathetic. He's stopped making dog jokes and I've stopped hoping for the job.

Philip has ignored me all week and instead has become friends with the other pinsetters. They stalk the lanes like a gang of thugs and make fun of the new kid, who is small-boned and unremarkable in the way that some young teenage boys can be. When I try to call Philip into the bar he turns his head and pretends to ignore me and his new friends laugh, full of themselves. He's even started calling Cindy the snack bar worker "Fatstuff" to her face when she refuses to give him his food for free. She's a tough one, though. She calls him "Fatstuff" back.

Tonight, while I'm carrying out buckets of margarita mix from the walk-in, Philip's mom walks in by herself. I'm used to seeing her with her girlfriend, and only on Thursdays, their league night. I expect her to come to the bar, to maybe talk about Philip and his recent bad behavior, but instead one of Bill's girls calls out "Shirley!" from back in the corner and Philip's mom walks directly to the corner to join the group. One of the women pulls out a chair for her and another actually stands up and hugs her before she sits.

I wipe down the taps and in the mirror I can see one of the women coming up to the bar, for a refill on their pitcher of margaritas.

"Better give us two," she calls out. She teeters in her high boots as she comes toward me.

"You sure?" I ask.

She reaches the bar and puts the plastic pitcher on top of the counter with a thud. Then she leans close to me. "Shirley was Bill's steady. Now she doesn't know what to do with herself. We're trying to keep up her spirits."

I'm about to ask about the girlfriend, the tattoo on the arm, but the woman in front of me shakes her French-braided head and says, "Don't even ask. It was a mess getting that woman out of her house. You don't want to know."

I mix up the pitchers and when the woman slides a twenty across the bar I tell her to keep it. My treat for Shirley. These women have created a story for Bill much better than my plots of murder, or terminal diseases. They make me feel like a sloppy amateur. Here they are, complete with costumes and condolences—here they are in their own personal soap opera. In the few weeks since the death, many of them have given themselves new identities. They're no longer the extras in the background of the scenes, watching while their husbands play the lead roles. The women have pushed their way in, and Shirley has cast herself as the heroine in this evolving drama.

"Thanks, doll." She carries the pitchers back to the table slowly, her long legs like stuffed sausages in tight black denim.

When Reg comes in an hour later, in full police uniform, complete with cap and gun holster, the girls have been cut off, but they aren't angry about it. They've invited me to sit at their table since it's been slow at the window. Instead, I call Gerald to see if he wants to come up and sit with me. Despite the fractals, we haven't slept together in over a week, and I'm lonely. I don't tell him this, though. I just say that I'm not feeling right and I'll make him free margaritas, my drink of the night. He says he'll try, but in the background I can hear a woman's laugh, or what sounds like a woman's laugh, and so I tell him to forget about stopping by.

"You pissed at me?" he asks. I tell him no, just bored, and hang up the phone. I realize I'm more upset than I thought I'd be. We're not serious, not even close, and I expected another woman to happen eventually, but I still feel stung with the realization that I'm not all he has. Or maybe I realize he's all I have. This makes me think of Philip, who is somewhere behind the lanes, with his new friends, probably drinking from a bottle of Jack Daniels one of them swiped when I was in the back changing a keg.

When Reg finally stands and comes behind the bar to pour his own Coke I give up. I close the window to the bar early for the night.

"You can't do that," Reg says.

"I just did." I walk out from behind the bar and sit at a stool next to him. "Besides, it's dead tonight." I look to see if he's carrying his pad of paper, his pen, and I think about the words underlined for emphasis. "How's the investigation?" I ask.

After the past week of stories, of lovers and drugs, I'm expecting something big. I am expecting stories of helicopters and middle-of-the-night raids, surveillance and night goggles. Instead, Reg gives me a confused look. "What investigation?"

"Bill's," I say.

Reg tilts back his head and finishes his Coke and I wait. "No investigation," he says, finally, and then wipes his sleeve across his mouth. His face is pink from the exertion of walking the lanes and he looks like a stuffed pig, juicy and tender. In his face I can see all of his nights like this, spent here at the lanes busting up fights in the parking lot.

"But what about the kid?" I ask.

"What kid?"

"Didn't he have a kid? In Lewisville?"

"Not as far as I can tell."

He sets his empty cup on the countertop in front of him and tosses his straw into the wastebasket beside him. "Look, people kill themselves all the time."

"But why did *he*?" I ask. I look over at the group of women in the corner. Two of them have their heads on the table, asleep, waiting for their husbands to finish their games and come to collect them to take them home to their kids, their oversized dogs waiting to be let out into the yard.

"Who knows?" he says. He must sense my disappointment because he puts his hand on my shoulder and apologizes. His touch is genuine, honest, the first real thing I've encountered at this place all week, and so I lay my head on his shoulder automatically and he lets me stay there a good long while.

The next morning, I get a call from a dog. Not a real dog, but the voice is the same as the one on the TV show. If this were a story, something I've made up, I'd at least give myself the editing job, the one I applied for, the one my degree qualifies me for. Instead, the dog tells me that that one has been filled, by someone with more experience, but they're willing to give me a lower-paying job in the writing department. Exploring new stories, new places in time, new characters from literature that a dog and his boy-master can visit. I ask why he's calling and not the woman I interviewed with, and he tells me his name is Jim, that he's the executive producer who is also the lead voice actor for the show. As he explains this I calculate the pay, and whether or not I can afford to live on that amount, and decide that it's worth the risk. Still, when I take the job and hang up, I don't feel as good as I think I should. Only two more weeks of the bowling alley, and Philip, and the men who stare at my chest and then tip me a nickel when they order their draft beers.

An hour later, when I see Philip's face through the peephole of the front door of my apartment, his face distorted, his smile a lopsided grimace, I almost don't let him in. I'm expecting a confrontation of some sort, his new friends probably waiting in the bushes beside my front door, their hands filled with eggs, rotten and ready to explode. I open the door anyway, expecting to be pummeled. I brace myself against the doorframe but it's just Philip, alone, the old Philip who looks sweet and kind and sad. He follows me inside my apartment and sits on the couch next to me, where he used to sit when he would come over after his mom kicked him out of the house for an afternoon and he had nowhere else to go. But that was a long time ago. He hasn't been over here in months. He looks down at his tennis shoes, which are black and leather and have some sort of pumping apparatus in the tongue. He doesn't speak, but he does finally look up at me. I wait.

"I brought something for you," he says. He slips his hand into his jacket and pulls out a piece of paper that has been folded into a small square. He unfolds it gently, carefully, and spreads it across his leg to smooth out the wrinkles. Then he stands up and hands it to me. He waits in front of me, his head down, while I read the only word written on the page: Faggot. The letters are written in a child's handwriting, printed letters that slant to the right, and when I look up to Philip, for an explanation, he sees that I don't understand.

"It's from Bill," he says. "It's a note I found in my locker. See the back? He wrote my name on it." I turn the piece of paper over and Philip's name is there in the same handwriting. Underneath Philip's name I can see a fine pencil mark, erased, a guide used to line up the letters, and this small erasure gives me a pain, and I hold the note back up for Philip to take.

He sits on the couch next to me, leans back, and sighs, and I drop the note onto the coffee table in front of us.

"Did you know my mom kicked her girlfriend out?"

"She came into the bar."

"Dee Dee did?"

"No, your Mom. Last night."

Philip seems relieved. "She ain't gay anymore. She told me."

I smile and stare at the word on the piece of paper on the table in front of us, at the childish writing, and wonder what it's supposed to mean.

"You're the only one I wanted to show this to," he says. He leans closer to me and I can smell that he's put on cologne. The sharp musk is cheap and awful, and my eyes start to water. He moves closer, puts his hand on the couch next to mine, and lets it rest there. His fingers are thick rigid sticks, unbent and unmoving.

"Why didn't you show this to your mom?" I put my hand over his so he won't lie and he looks up into my eyes and I can still see the old Philip there, kind and willing, but I see the new anger there too. The hard look in his eyes that he's had since the new boy was hired in and became the punching bag and Philip finally became one of the pinsetters.

"I ain't gay," he says, finally, and he pushes my hand away and stands up.

"I never said you were," I say, but I remember Philip confessing that he'd let a boy kiss him, once, while they were at a tournament in San Angelo. I never told him I thought that kiss meant he was gay, but told him that it was okay if he were. But he probably told me about the kiss on one of the first nights I got together with

Gerald, though, and so I didn't pay much attention. I was thinking about Gerald's mouth on mine, his hands flat against my stomach.

Now I want to pay attention to him—I want things to go right. But when I go to stand up Philip pins my shoulders back against the couch with a strength that is surprising.

"That's enough," I tell him. I try to laugh but the sound catches in my throat and comes out as a whine instead.

He tightens his fingers around my upper arms and keeps me pinned down.

"Stop," I say, and I feel like I'm only imagining his fingers gripped around both of my upper arms. But I can feel them, digging into the muscle, the meat, already forming deep bruises.
I know that this situation could get out of hand in a second, in the brief moment it would take me to scream, and I think about how I would write this violent coming-of-age scene for a costumed dog and his boy-master, but none of the stories of betrayal I flip through seem to fit. *Hamlet? A Tale of Two Cities?*

So instead I say something completely ridiculous. "I'll call your mother," I say. I try to remember the first time Philip was here, in my apartment, on my couch, and I remember when he was twelve and I was watching him while his parents were gone for the day at a bowling tournament in Waco.

He lets go of my arms and stands up and closes his eyes. "Fuck you," he says, his voice almost a whisper. Then he walks across the room and out the front door. He leaves it open, and I wait for him to come back in, by himself or with the other pinsetters, who I am sure are waiting for him outside, in the parking lot, drinking beer and listening to loud, thumping music. But I don't move. I sit right where I am and I wait for them.

In my ending, Gerald shows up and takes me in his arms and lets me sink against his chest while he holds me and strokes my hair, and kisses the side of my face, not in the angry way he kisses me on the mouth, but in a soft way, in gentle brushes that almost put me to sleep. I am not alone on my couch, with the yells of violent teenagers outside my front door, in the parking lot. Before they drive off in an angry burst, in a flurry of tire squeals and stereo bass, I hear an explosion of beer bottles hit the brick wall next to the front door of my apartment. I sit on my couch, the bruises not yet coming to the surface of my skin, and try to make some sort of meaning out of the scatter of green glass decorating the cement breezeway that separates my apartment from the parking lot.

The Monkey Woman Who Married the Alligator Boy Makes A Comeback

Sometimes the kids from the neighborhood watch them through the windows. Priscilla keeps the curtains drawn whenever she can, but when there's a breeze it's hard not to crank the panels open and air things out. She'll get up early to make Art's coffee and they'll be there, three kids with their faces pressed to the wide window behind the kitchen table. The kids have no fear. They keep their faces pressed against the glass until Priscilla goes to the front door to open it and shoo them from the yard. Only then do they run down the alley that snakes through the backs of the houses, the one littered with trashcans and forgotten sports equipment, or behind the trailer that's parked on the side of the house, the one Art and Priscilla used to travel with and the one the neighbors now want to be towed away. The trailer that has exaggerated, cartoonish pictures of them painted on the side, pictures where both of them are in cages, baring dangerous canines and looking like beasts, above which are their names: *Monkey Woman and Alligator Boy*.

But the kids don't run until they're made to. They'll stand forever looking in through the kitchen window and watch Art read the paper; or Priscilla, dressed in her bathrobe and slippers, making pancakes and biscuits and sausage patties. Priscilla and Art ignore them, but it's hard to concentrate with neighborhood kids watching everything you do. They see everything and then they whisper, the shells of their hands blocking their mouths as they talk to each other.

Priscilla and Art go to the mall a lot now since their retirement, to buy Levi's for Arthur or for tools for the yard when there's a sale on Craftsman at Sears. Sometimes they hold hands, Priscilla careful to avoid the sores that cover each of Art's knuckles and the blisters that bubble at the tips of his fingers. These pearlescent orbs have always reminded Priscilla of tiny onions, and they've never quite healed, even with the medicated ointment she rubs carefully into them each night. The smell of the ointment is like Listerine and peppermint toothpaste and it's the smell she's come to associate with touch, with his touch, which is like sand on her skin. Even so, the ointment wears off. There's always a pile of scales on her pillow each morning, dull in the light from the window. She reads these flaky scales like Braille, arranges them into words that carry the two of them to an island, or a forest deep in the wilderness of Alaska.

Someplace far away from the suburbs of Tampa, someplace without fast food restaurants, lawns to mow, malls to go to when they need ointment and jeans and power tools.

At the mall, the Norms stare at Priscilla and Art when they pause to look at the displays in the storefront windows. Priscilla wears a caftan covered with large, bright flowers that falls loose against her. The edges of her body are blurred underneath the material; her chest is large, sure, but it's the hair at her neck the Norms stare at. The fur covers nearly every inch of her body, a soft black that creeps up her neck and covers her cheeks, her forehead, the sliver of space above her lip. The hair at her temples is going gray, but she's delighted that the rest has stayed as it's been all her life. It sometimes occurs to Priscilla that she's dressed like a child, in her brightly colored smocks, but she allows herself this indulgence of flamboyance since Art always asks her to wear the thick body stocking that covers most of the hair, and the polyester fabric is flesh-colored and tight and sticks to her skin. After walking around in the stocking all day, Priscilla sweats so much that when she pulls the thing off at night, there's an odor like a zoo that fills the room. She has to hand-wash the expensive stocking nightly with Woolite, in the bathroom sink.

Then there's Arthur and his beautiful face like the aging actor Priscilla sees in the orange juice commercial they play during *Wheel of Fortune*, the one with the tanned face and toothy grin that's a little lopsided. But from Art's neck down, there are the scales, which are pale blue, sometimes green if you look at them in the right light. Smooth like a fish but his family always thought alligator sounded more threatening and drew in more crowds, so 'Alligator Boy' is the name his uncle stuck him with. The family put him in a giant fish tank and had him float around like a child's swim toy and all that chlorine and sun started his skin peeling and the shedding hasn't stopped since.

So they get stares at the Crosswinds Mall from the big-haired girls who stand around Itza Pretzel and flirt with the blond-haired kid whose pants are always slipping off his rear end, the blond boy whose stare always lasts a little longer than it should and is always a little meaner than everyone else's. And today, when Art and Priscilla walk by on their way to Sears (for an electric screwdriver; Art's putting together bookshelves for Priscilla's antique doll collection), there's a new boy working the pretzel place, too. A boy with brown hair. Much nicer looking, Priscilla thinks, than *Mister Buttocks*. He pretends not to stare, but Priscilla can feel his eyes on the backs of her legs when they go past and she tries to pretend, for once, that she's just the same as any of the other middle-aged housewives roaming the food court, dressed in their velour tracksuits and tennis whites. Priscilla's not so old; her legs are nice. She can still fit into her costume, which was a little tight on her even back when she performed. The sequins always popped off whenever she bent over onstage, but the crowds loved that. After her show, she and Art sat on their bed and counted their money at night, in the dim light of their trailer, like thieves. Back then, they could afford to do what they wanted and every dollar collected meant freedom for them—from Art's family, Priscilla's mother, the cruel teenagers who sometimes threw rocks at them when they walked through the town after the carnival closed for the night.

Today at the mall, the new Pretzel Boy pushes his way through the group of women with strollers who've congregated outside of the Gap like a brood of hens, their necks bent together and heads bowed in gossip. He pushes through and stands in front of Priscilla and Arthur and hands them each a flyer good for a free pretzel. He shifts from one foot to the other and Priscilla thinks she recognizes the boy, recognizes the way he pushes the hair off of his forehead and away from his eyes. Art recognizes him, too.

"The paper boy," Art says. "You used to bring the paper." And Priscilla remembers putting money into the boy's palm, folding the bills and wrapping his fingers around them to keep the money from flying away with the wind.

"Sixteen now, though," the boy says. "Got a real job. A car, too, and a girl." He turns and points back to one of the big-haired girls who stand in front of Itza Pretzel. "The blonde one," he tells them. "With the mini skirt." Priscilla squints to see and there are two girls, both wearing short glowing skirts. One holds a pink pouf of cotton candy, her fingers buried in the top of the mound. The other has her long, thin arm draped around the shoulders of the blond boy with the pants. As if on cue, they all turn at the same time and stare. When the Pretzel Boy tries to wave the group over, they all burst out in a combustion of laughter.

Art takes Priscilla's arm and they walk to Sears, at the other end of the mall. Today Priscilla tries on bras while Art shops for paint to cover over their pictures on the side of the trailer. The bras make Priscilla's breasts look like bullets, like things made of steel, but she's promised Art that she'll wear one when they go out in public, under her stocking, and so she tries one on in every color they have, every shade of nude and tan and beige they have hanging on the rack, the entire flesh-toned rainbow display of bras, which is the only color of rainbow available, apparently, to women with breasts larger than a child.

At home that night, Priscilla takes a long bath, then scoops the hair from the drain. She does this for Arthur, so he won't scream that the tub's clogging up when he takes his shower in the morning. When she climbs into bed next to Arthur, she smoothes the scales from her pillow and leans in close to him.

When Priscilla's on top of him, Art slips his fingers inside of her. Priscilla sees white light when this happens, a moment of brightness in the dark room. And then she touches him, fingers the scales that cover his chest, the tops of his shoulders. They move their fingers around each other's bodies as if they're pointing out countries on a map, ones ready for invasion. They do this until they're both too tired to keep their eyes open. Even then they wind down slowly, keeping their hands going until they're fast asleep.

On Saturday, there are Jeeps parked all over the mall. Actually inside the mall, parallel parked between potted ferns. Priscilla and Art put their hands on the red one parked in front of Itza Pretzel. Priscilla's hands leave wet prints on the slick paint when she steps away from the Jeep. She looks at the options listed on the price sticker that is glued to the window. Almost thirty thousand dollars for something that would surely kill them if they went on the highway, at least here in South Florida. Still, Priscilla wants one. Only because it's something they can't afford. When they were traveling, they were never rich, but at least they made their own money and they spent it as they wanted—on clothes, a fancy trailer to travel in, dolls for Priscilla's collection. Now their money comes from the government, who has classified them both as disabled, and they budget their money every month on the computer Art insisted they needed. Art prints out their budget each month and Priscilla always aches when she sees those lines and red numbers on the spreadsheet. Apparently, they have enough for food and for the house and almost nothing else, certainly not a shiny new convertible. Those new car displays are for the normal-bodied teenagers whose parents buy them under the condition that the kids work at the mall to pay for gas.

Art takes his hands away from the Jeep's smooth side panel slowly and there are no palm prints at all—only a few scales fall to the floor. Priscilla steps over them, then rubs them into the tile with the heel of her flip flop. Behind them, in front of Itza Pretzel, the brown-haired Pretzel Boy stands with a tray of pretzel chunks stabbed with toothpicks. He sees Priscilla and turns away, but she grabs Art's arm and pulls him over to the boy with the tray. The boy holds the tray up so that Art can look over the samples. He takes two and hands one to Priscilla. The Pretzel Boy looks nervous today, keeps looking over his shoulder at the blond kid who's working behind the counter. The kids behind the counter are laughing, their faces red and shining in the glow of the heat lamps. Priscilla looks around for the big-haired girls, but they're not here today. Maybe it's too early; they're still in bed. Art takes more samples and drops the toothpicks. The Pretzel Boy looks at Priscilla's neck, at the hair that creeps out of the rim of her body stocking. "You used to shave it," he says. His face goes red, too. "When I brought your paper, you didn't have any on your face."

"Electrolysis. Gave me a rash and it grew back, anyway. What's the point? I grow hair."

Art walks away to look at a luggage set in the window of Paradise Leather. The backs of his calves shine iridescent in the sun from the massive skylights that run the length of the mall. "My friend," the Pretzel Boy says, "my friend was wondering if you're still in shows."

"Not for a few years," she says. "The state closed us down." She considers telling him the whole story, about the young teenage amputee in the wheelchair who went to a show outside of St. Petersburg and saw a freak with no legs and got upset because the freak's body looked too much like her own new body and then her lawyer Daddy decided to do something about that.

"Because of the trailer I thought maybe you guys still did them." Pretzel Boy looks back over his shoulder at the blond kid who's still laughing and is now shaking his head, egging him on. "Cause he says he'd pay. To see you. You know, without all the clothes on."

Priscilla stares at the blond kid. He looks like all of the teenagers who live on their street, in their neighborhood. She imagines he drives a loud car with a good deal of exhaust. She imagines he drives really fast, smokes and drinks and can still find a hand to switch gears with.

Priscilla walks away from the Pretzel Boy. This is never how she thought her comeback would be, in a peep show for a bunch of horny teens. She considers herself an artist, a woman with a gift. She had her own show once and she could *dance*. Art said she was the most beautiful woman he had ever seen, and before she met him, no one had ever looked at her and said that. And even if she didn't believe him—not completely—when she performed, when she was on stage and the overhead lights made the skin on her arms glisten, that was when she felt the power she had, if not the beauty. Her shows were always a sell out. The Norms would crowd the stage as she twirled in front of them, and the brave ones—the ones who pushed to the front of the crowd—would reach out their hands to touch the hair on her feet, the flash of white skin at her ankles.

At Sears, Priscilla follows Art to the automotive department. They need a new battery for the Ford. Art closely inspects the solid black boxes, looking for scrapes or inconsistencies, as if it would be just their luck to get the one faulty battery in the bunch. Just their luck to buy the one that would blow them up when Art turned the ignition. Art points to stickers pasted to the tops of the batteries that announce how long the battery can be expected to last. He calculates months into years and Priscilla notices that his fingers are getting worse. Today there are blisters on the tops of each hand, too, fresh and pink.

"Five years," Art says. "Seven."

While Art pays for the battery, Priscilla watches a commercial on one of the televisions in electronics, except the sound to the television this commercial is showing on is down low and all she can hear are the cheers from a basketball game playing on one of the other televisions. It's a car commercial and a beautiful blonde woman is maneuvering a shiny black Cadillac around highway curves that suddenly turn into a cartoon landscape. The road becomes a pen and ink sketch and so do the mountains around her, the clouds. Everything but the woman and the car. When this transformation happens, the cheers on the other television grow louder. Something important is happening in the basketball game, something wonderful and amazing, but Priscilla watches the woman drive her way right through that artificial sunset until the commercial ends abruptly and the car disappears.

At home the kids are waiting. They are pressed against the kitchen window, as usual, and they're small against the house. When they see the Ford pull up, they pretend they're retrieving a soccer ball from the bushes. One of the kids tucks the half-deflated thing under his arm and they go away; the three of them go slowly behind the trailer on the side of the house. Art painted over half of the trailer, the half with his snarling smile and menacing eyes, and Priscilla's picture is the only one left. In the portrait she holds a banana and has sharp teeth. Ridiculous. But already she misses Arthur's and something heavy seems to drop against her chest, quickens the rhythm of her heart.

"You'd think they'd be bored with us by now," Art says. "What's the big deal?"

Inside, Priscilla boils water for macaroni and cheese. Art sits at the kitchen table, waiting. Priscilla brings him a bag of potato chips and he eats them slowly, one thin chip at a time. She sits across from him and tells him about the Pretzel Boy. About his friend's offer. Art's hands shine greasy with oil and Priscilla watches them light up when the sun comes in through the window. She can tell what Art is thinking by the way he holds one hand over the other. He's upset.

"These kids have no manners at all," Art tells her. "You'd think they were raised by wolves. What kind of parents do these kids have?"

Priscilla reaches out and puts her hand on top of Art's. She's still sweating from walking in the body stocking and when she pulls her hand away to wipe her palms against the front of her shirt Art stops her, then covers the tops of her hands with his own. "Those kids at the mall are bullies, plain and simple." He slides his thumb across the ridges of Priscilla's knuckles to calm her. "They say anything to you again, I'll give them a piece of my mind."

Priscilla lowers her eyes to the table and creates a pattern from the scales next to her arm. "It's not them I'm upset about, really," she says. "It's not having a show. I want to perform again, Art."

Art's hand jerks away from hers and when Priscilla finally looks up she sees that Art's eyes are narrowed. But then his face goes soft.

"There's no way I'm going to let you make a fool of yourself," he tells her.

"Why can't we find a place to rent and do things our own way?" Priscilla's voice is quiet and she thinks she might start to cry. There's a tightness in her chest and she bites her lip. "What about one of those little warehouse spaces off of Grimble?"

"What do you think those kids are interested in? Your dancing?"

"Your brother could help us with the permits," Priscilla tells him.

"This is ridiculous," Art says. "You're fifty years old."

Priscilla lowers her eyes to the table and settles them on the small scattering of bread crumbs leftover from Art's breakfast.

"Forget it, Priscilla." Art's voice is full of anger. "You're not making a fool of yourself."

"Why would I be making a fool of myself?"

"You would be."

"Says who?" Priscilla crosses her arms and lifts her head.

"Enough is enough. Now stop this."

Art pulls back his hands which Priscilla knows means the discussion is over. The kids are at the window, watching, and Priscilla turns to face them. She's upset, her eyes are watering and the kids laugh and stick their tongues out against the glass. Circles of steam surround their faces and their eyes grow big when Priscilla goes to the window and pulls the curtains closed. One of the kids, the one with the soccer ball, gives her the finger before he runs away.

That night, Art washes Priscilla's back. He sits on the edge of the pink bathtub and leans over her with a sponge. The flesh colored body stocking balled at his feet on the linoleum floor, he avoids her eyes as he skims small handfuls of fur off the top of the water. This shedding has never happened before, not like this, and tonight, hunched over and crying, she lets out moans that make her sound like a wounded animal. She imagines the spaces on her back, perhaps between her shoulder blades, of smooth skin, patchy white gaps in the lake of black hair. Priscilla knows that the eucalyptus oil in the water stings Art's hands, but he says nothing. They are coming apart, she thinks. Or maybe transforming.

Art helps Priscilla from the bath, and he wraps her in a towel, then puts her into bed, between the cool dotted sheets.

"I love you," he says. He curls in beside her, buries his face in her back. With the tips of his fingers he touches the white spaces.

"I want things to be the way they used to," Priscilla says.

"Those kids'll stop coming around when school starts in a couple of weeks." Art pulls his hand away and tucks it under his pillow, settles his head before he closes his eyes to sleep. "They're just bored."

Priscilla sighs and stares at the ceiling, at the swirls of plaster that constellate the room. This transformation is a punishment, Priscilla thinks. For what, she doesn't know.

Priscilla begins to feel comfort at the mall. She starts to go alone, without Art. She wakes early in the morning, takes the Ford and drives the back roads, through the housing developments that spill children onto the streets. She drives slowly and looks at the sprawling ranches set back from the road. Behind each closed door she imagines families having breakfast, oatmeal and fruit smoothies, watching TV. Morning cartoons with characters shaped like an extended finger, or a short stubby toe. Covered in purple and red fur, these creatures dance to the rhythmic music the human deejay plays on his boombox. She waits behind a school bus carrying kids to day camp and links each child to a house on the block. The blonde girl with braids belongs to the white sprawler on the corner. The boy with the blue backpack goes with the red brick across the street.

At the mall, she memorizes the color-coded map. Each store has a number and a color to let you know how to find it. Itza Pretzel is purple 228. The size of the store is small compared to those that surround it; the shape is perfectly square. She avoids the Pretzel Boy and sticks to the lower level. She wanders into almost every store, at least briefly, and allows herself to buy one small item each day, something she can hide in her purse. A lipstick. A pair of earrings. A comb.

She lets the people stare, but soon they're used to her and nobody looks. She wanders through the crowds like anyone else, like any other middle-aged woman dressed like a child. She sweats under the body stocking. The heat is relentless; it's late summer and in the nineties, but the air-conditioned mall is always the same—the temperature a constant seventy-three degrees.

When Priscilla gets walking, the friction from the stocking causes heat and she's left damp under the layers. When this happens she buys a Coke at the frozen yogurt shop and sits on a bench in the middle of the mall, on the lower level. There's always something grand on display in this area, and for the past month the center has been filled with giant sandcastles over ten feet tall. Priscilla sits and sips her Coke and waits for one of them to crumble. It's only a matter of time, she thinks, a matter of waiting. One day she'll show up and one of the intricately designed towers will have been reduced to a hump of sand and she'll be sorry she missed the fall.

She avoids the pretzel place, but one day she comes out of Sears and sees him. The Pretzel Boy is standing outside the CD store, waiting for someone. He sees Priscilla and waves. She feels trapped, suddenly exposed. She's an animal caught in the headlights and when he runs up to her, blocking her escape to the entrance of *Nothing But Jewelry!*, which Priscilla can see just off to her right, she is left still in front of him, unable to move. The Pretzel Boy's face shines in the glare of the overhead skylights and he flashes white teeth. He looks eager, happy, ready to please.

"About what I said that one time," he tells her. "I'm sorry. My friend made me ask. He's sort of a jerk." The Pretzel Boy has cut his hair short and Priscilla gets a good look at his eyes. They are large and the most incredible shade of brown, framed with long lashes. He looks right at her face without turning away and Priscilla is touched.

"It's not that big of a deal." She lowers her eyes to the ground, a little embarrassed.

The Pretzel Boy lifts his hand and wraps his fingers gently around Priscilla's arm. "It was," he says, "and, hey, yeah, sorry." He keeps his hand on Priscilla's arm and she looks at the thin, white fingers against her dark hair. His hands are soft and beautiful, and when she looks up, the Pretzel Boy smiles. His front teeth overlap and the top of his lip catches before it pulls up.

"It's okay," Priscilla says, "really."

"I just asked because he dared me to and I didn't want to look like a chicken, you know?" The Pretzel Boy pulls his hand away and rubs the top of his head.

"Your haircut looks nice," Priscilla says, and the boy smiles and lifts up his shoulders. He kicks the toe of one of his sneakered feet against the top of the other.

"So you're not mad or anything?" He looks over her shoulder, at the sandcastles, and then he looks down.

"Of course not," Priscilla says.

The Pretzel Boy smiles, then turns away from her. "Cool," he says, "that makes me feel better." He lifts his hand and waves, then starts to walk away from her, and Priscilla feels the need to say something else to him. She feels, suddenly, like a smitten schoolgirl. She knows this is ridiculous, that the boy is a child, really. She looks at the back of the boy's head, at the dark hair streaked with gold, and thinks of Art, alone at home, watching *The Price is Right*. She thinks of Art as a teenager, and the way he must have kept his body hidden. And then she remembers her own body, her teenage body, when the hair began to grow over her chest, up her neck, and over her face like a disease. She had hidden her body, too. And now here she is, an adult, married to a man she knows she wouldn't be able to live without, stuffed into a body stocking and standing in the middle of a mall, surrounded by women with baby strollers and shopping bags. She is a woman in the suburbs whose neighbors want her to feel shame, whose husband has done his best to make them fit in.

"Tonight," she tells him. "Come to my house, to the window on the side." She says this forcefully, a command. The strength in her voice surprises her.

The Pretzel Boy turns back to her, a curious look on his face, in his eyes, and Priscilla walks away from him. She feels, for the first time in months, like herself. She feels the Pretzel Boy watching her and she wishes that she didn't have the flesh colored stocking under her dress. She has the desire to feel exposed, finally, completely revealed.

That night, Art comes to her. The curtains are parted and a thin stream of light shines through the window and lights up the scales on his arms, his legs. They have not touched each other in weeks and if he notices that the curtains are open he says nothing. Priscilla has not told him that they are there, watching. That she was outside with them only a few minutes ago, taking their money. Wadded wet bills that they pulled from the pockets of their jeans, from their jackets.

She is naked on the bed, waiting. She wonders about the teenagers outside and what they are thinking. That her body is disgusting. That she and Art are freaks and there is nothing at all beautiful about them. But Priscilla imagines that she and Art are far away and that Art is coming to her on a deserted beach and he is the man from the orange juice commercial, all white teeth and tanned skin. Priscilla is the woman who drives the Cadillac into a cartoon. The two of them are not in this room or this house or this neighborhood full of mean children. They are not themselves.

Art stands in front of her and holds out his arms. In the dark, his hands are not the ones that she knows. They are beautiful, without the blisters that rough the smooth surface. They do not have the smell of his touch, his peppermint ointment.

"You are amazing," Art tells her. "Amazing. Amazing."

And their touching, the two of them together in their fur and scales, their shedding bodies—feels different tonight. Their touching feels like it used to, back in the beginning, before they got dismissed to this planned community neighborhood full of rules and regulations, expensive sports cars and nosy children.

And then he is inside of her and they're together again, with the light coming in just right from the window, and they know what it's like to live with their bodies.

Jimmy and Mary at Home Plate

When Mary squinted, Jimmy looked like a brown-green blur at second base, a lump of something ridiculous and ugly in the swarm of white-clad ballplayers loosening up their arms and stretching their hamstrings. Then she heard the whistle and Mary opened her eyes and Jimmy came to her, came running slow and lopey, the foam taco suit he wore forcing his arms up and away from his body. Mary stood behind third base and waved her arms in front of her chest, a signal for Jimmy to hurry and stumble around the bases more efficiently. The kid chasing him tonight was fast and if Jimmy didn't pick up the pace he was going to get tackled before they even got to the third base bag, nowhere close to home plate. The kid was eight or nine years old, a chubby boy with a batting helmet slipping over his eyes, a light blue little league jersey dusty with orange field dirt too big and sliding off one of his shoulders.

But Jimmy picked up the pace, and when he rounded third he came close to Mary and she could see his dark eyes and the whites around them, through the meshy screen embedded in the part of the suit that covered the top half of his face. He pushed off the base with his right foot and then flailed toward home plate. The kid was even closer now, and as he ran he held his arms out in front of him, trying to reach the back of the giant taco in front of him. Jimmy the Puffy Taco, almost to home plate, slowed down enough that the kid pounced on him, tackling him before Jimmy could stretch his leg out to slide dramatically home. When the umpire jerked his thumb over his head, exaggerating the tag-out, the kid jumped up, arms over his head, triumphant. Jimmy leaned up and whispered something to the kid and, for a second, the kid looked confused. But then he bent his knees and his elbows and danced. The kid closed his eyes and scooted around Jimmy, kicking the dust up in little clouds so Mary could only see Jimmy's legs for an instant. Then Jimmy was off the ground and the crowd clapped for the kid who was now running to claim his prize—a massive five-pound Hershey's chocolate bar—from the announcer in front of the visitors' dugout.

The umpire was waving her off the field and Mary, eyes watery from the dust and the lights, back-pedaled down into the Missions' dugout. She stepped over the batting helmets that were tossed around the wooden bench and to the back near the door to the locker room to wait for Jimmy to come off the field. The players

Jimmy came down into the dugout finally, his fingers gripped around the railings by the stairs for support. One of the players followed him off the field and pushed past him and Jimmy fell back. He held one arm out and swayed until he regained his balance.

"Asshole," Jimmy muttered. The word came out muffled through the mesh screen, a blur of vowels. "Did you see that?"

"Of course I did," Mary said. "I'm standing right in front of you." Mary waved her hand in front of the screen that covered Jimmy's eyes and he batted her hand away, then stepped past her and made his way to the back of the dugout.

Mary held open the door to the locker room and the two of them walked through the empty room and back up to the stadium. The stadium was new and beautiful, all clean white concrete and metal chairs painted blue. In left field there weren't any chairs, just a nice patch of green grass where people brought blankets and sat in the sun with their coolers and kids.

When Mary and Jimmy emerged from the locker room, a swarm of kids pulled at him, tugging at his costume and chasing him away from Mary until he was a blur of brown and green going around a corner.

Mary ducked behind the souvenir stand and the beer vendor who was set up under a bright blue awning. She went around the stadium and then through the chain link gate that opened onto the patch of green at left field. She sat cross-legged on the grass and watched the insects buzz under the stadium lights. She wore a tank top and her arms were coated with a thin film of dried salt that dusted off under her fingers. It had been over one hundred degrees that evening and the heat still hovered in the stadium like an afterthought.

A player from the opposing team hit a home run and Mary caught a glimpse of Jimmy's taco suit as he emerged from the Missions' dugout to lead the crowd in a round of "boos." Jimmy waved his arms and people in the stands stomped their feet and the vibrations went through Mary's body, settling into her bones. A crowd of children gathered at the top of the Missions' dugout and began yelling at Jimmy. These were the kids that followed him around the stadium, the ones who pulled pieces off the taco suit and ran away, the brown and green foam chunks small trophies that they clasped in their fists and raised over their heads.

Mary sat until the game was over and after the crowd had filed out into the parking lot, she waited with a group of teenage girls outside the door to the players' locker room. Some of them were players' wives but most of them were prowlers. The wives stood to the side of the group and frowned at the teenage girls, who all seemed to wear the exact same uniform of tank-top and cut-off denim shorts. It was cap night at the ballpark and most of the girls had theirs on, blonde ponytails looped through the back opening. When the players started to come out, freshly showered and dressed in jeans, the girls took their hats off and held them out to the players to sign.

Jimmy eventually emerged from the locker room and Mary went to him while the girls stayed around the door. He pushed through the crowd and was suddenly normal again, a doughy guy in tan cargo shorts and a Budweiser T-shirt. Sometimes, after a win, he would emerge from the locker room in his taco suit to celebrate with the fans and Mary would wait for him while he shuffled through the crowds, hands raised for high-fives. On those nights she'd drive home and he'd lie across the backseat, the taco suit filling the back window like some sort of contaminated sunset.

The prowlers always ignored him. They probably thought he was a trainer, or a writer for the paper. Tonight they pushed past him to get a glimpse into the opened locker room door, anticipation brightening their young faces. Mary held Jimmy's hand and they walked together out of the stadium and across the small pedestrian bridge to the players' lot.

"Let's go get a beer," Jimmy sighed. "I'm in desperate need. I was terrible tonight. Everything went wrong."

Jimmy squeezed her hand and Mary tried to think of something to say. One of his flip flops slid off and he stopped to pick it up. His T-shirt slid up his back when he bent over and Mary stared at the pale strip of skin between his frayed hem and the elastic band of his underwear. He looked too large, too past his expiration date, and she suspected that the charm she had felt the first night he had put on the taco suit was starting to fade. He stood up slowly, his hand bracing his side. He winced.

"Did you forget your brace again?" Mary crossed her arms over her chest and waited for Jimmy to look at her. He turned away from her without answering, though, and Mary followed him to the car. As he walked, she stared at the backs of his legs and wondered when he had grown so large. There were little pockets of fat behind each of his knees and Mary looked down at her own legs. They were bigger, too. The insides of her thighs rubbed together in the heat and red patches had blossomed from the friction. When she got to the car, Jimmy was leaning against the passenger door, staring back at the glowing stadium.

"I think you were great tonight," Mary told him. She said nothing about the pockets of fat, or the way they were suddenly changing, both of them. "The kids loved you."

Jimmy turned away from the glowing disc of the stadium and opened his mouth. He started to say something, but stopped. "I try," he said, giving in. "I really do." Mary knew he was thinking of the plans he'd made earlier that day to meet up with his uncle and cousins later that night, midnight poker he knew she hated but would sneak out for later, after she'd fallen asleep. The beer, the queso. The bags of greasy chips he'd paw his way through.

The inside of the car exhaled a heat that hit them both in a large wave when they opened the doors. The sky had darkened but the night was still hot and dry and exhausted them both.

As Mary wove her way around the remaining cars, scattered like broken teeth around the exit to the lot, Jimmy dug through the glove compartment until he found the motivational tape he listened to every afternoon on his way to work and slid it into the stereo. He turned up the volume until Mary slapped his hand and he turned the knob back a little. He tapped the dashboard with his fingers and Mary concentrated on the white line at the edge of the highway on-ramp as she drove. *You need to be aware that who you are ultimately depends on how others see you, the voice on the tape warned. Surround yourself with the kind of people you want to become.*

The next morning, Jimmy came into the kitchen, a little hungover and rubbing the sides of his head. He wore boxer shorts and his stomach traveled over the top of the waistband, a white wave patched with black hairs. Mary had been asleep when he came in the night before, but she could feel the weight of him in bed when she woke up. He went to the refrigerator, opened the door, and stared inside. He sighed.

"What time do you work this afternoon?" Mary shuffled the newspaper that sat on the kitchen table in front of her and took a sip of coffee. She tried to ignore the leg that wobbled the table and allowed coffee rings to pool underneath her mug.

"Five, but I might show up late. Tell Henry I had some errands." Jimmy opened the refrigerator and stared inside, the look on his face hopeful, as if expecting a spread of leftovers to suddenly appear, the foil domed covers twinkling in the dim light. "Wait, no," he said. "Tell him I had to go help Mom with her shots."

When Jimmy was hungover, Mary felt sorry for him. Henry, Jimmy's uncle, owned the Mexican restaurant where they both waited tables and was the one who made Jimmy dress as a Puffy Taco to promote the restaurant's house special, the puffed taco platter, which consisted of three oily taco balls plopped into the middle of a field of bright orange rice.

Two months ago, when Jimmy came to her in their bedroom after his first baseball game, still dressed in his taco suit with the foam lettuce fraying in a line down his chest, Mary felt her heart open up to him like it had when they first started dating. She stood and put her hands on the foam and felt his warmth coming through to her, and in that moment she felt that she could love him passionately again. He looked ridiculous—a grown man dressed up as a taco, standing in front of her ready for sex. She felt she could love him passionately again until he slipped the foam outfit over his head and stood in front of her, naked except for the brown tights, chest and face covered with sweat. Then the growing feeling for him got thrown in the corner on the chair with the foam suit and when he lowered himself on top of her she'd closed her eyes and concentrated on the feel of the mattress springs against her back. "I love you!" he'd said. He'd whispered it with enthusiasm into the side of her face.

Mary spent the early afternoon drinking coffee and cleaning the apartment, and Jimmy stayed in bed reading the paper. He had the pages spread out over the comforter around him and he shuffled them noisily while Mary cleaned the kitchen and the bathroom, a headache strumming her temples. At three, she took a shower and dressed in her white blouse and black skirt.

"I'm leaving," she called into the bedroom.

"Okay." Jimmy sounded half-asleep and Mary knew that he would stay there in bed and she'd have to think up some lie to tell Henry, who would follow her around the back kitchen asking where Jimmy was and if he knew he was scheduled to close up the restaurant that night. Henry was a big man, over six feet tall and at least three hundred pounds. He was always angry and sweating, and just the sound of his voice scared Mary. He was nothing like Jimmy, who was quiet and shy and hardly ever yelled.

But Henry never came out of the kitchen that night, and Jimmy never showed up to close the restaurant. When Mary's shift was over, she wiped down her tables, filled her salt and pepper shakers, and stuffed her apron and order pads into the locker she shared with Jimmy. She slipped out the back door unnoticed.

The note said that he was at the hospital with his mother. His car keys were on the table next to the note and there was also a burrito still wrapped in Henry's signature-style paper, the oil seeped through and leaking in spots on the edge of the note. Jimmy's handwriting was tiny enough that Mary had to turn on the overhead light in the kitchen to read the note. She read it twice and wondered what he wanted her to do. Then the phone rang.

"Where have you been?" Jimmy's voice was loud and high. "I went to the restaurant to pick you up."

"I went for a beer, to cool off." Mary stretched the phone cord and went over to the window air conditioner that was set up over the sink. She cranked the dial to 'high' and pulled her shirt up to let the air blow across her stomach. She felt bloated and tired, her arms and legs too weighty. "I don't feel so good," she said.

"I'm at the hospital. They think Mom's had a stroke."

Mary felt guilty then. After she'd read the note she'd assumed the hospital trip with Jimmy's mother was just another minor emergency with her diabetes, like the time last month when she forgot her insulin. "Is she okay?"

"No, she's not okay." Jimmy's voice cracked and Mary could tell that he'd started to cry. "Jesus, I'm sorry."

"I'll come up."

But his mother was at a hospital she'd never been to before, and Mary didn't recognize the hospital's name, so Jimmy gave her directions in a tired voice, a series of streets named after presidents, punctuated with *easts* and *wests*. Mary tried to write the directions down quickly, exactly as he gave them, then gave up and just drew arrows.

When she hung up the phone she thought of Jimmy, sitting in the hospital room, holding his mother's hand, the tears running down his face, his neck. His mother's diabetes kept her sick, though she'd never had to spend a full night in the hospital since Mary had known her. Usually, she'd feel faint or her vision would blur, and she'd have a neighbor take her into the emergency room and the doctors would check her blood sugar and lecture her on her diet, the cans of Coors that she couldn't give up. Then she'd call Jimmy and tell him she was dying. His mother would say it over and over, quietly, between Jimmy's questions, until he started to cry and had to hang up the phone. Jimmy's mother was Henry's sister, and when she'd come to the restaurant, she'd get seated in Mary's section and would tell Henry how many mistakes Mary had made with her order, how the rice was cold, the beans too oily, until she finally went back to the kitchen and fixed her own meal. Mary stayed at home when Jimmy went to visit her, in the old ranch house from the 1950's in the rambling subdivision across the highway where she lived.

Mary felt suddenly nauseous and had to run to the bathroom. Her eyes watered and she threw up repeatedly until she curled into a ball on the cool tiled floor of the bathroom and heaved up air.

Jimmy's mother was a mess of tubes and tape, her nose and mouth plugged with plastics and rubber. Jimmy and his uncle (who still wore his Henry's apron, splattered with orange grease) sat on either side of her bed, not touching anything and staring at the floor. Mary came in and they both looked up, surprised to see her. Jimmy coughed.

"I got lost," Mary said. "I ended up in the Southside somewhere."

Henry shook his head and turned away, but Jimmy stood and came to her. He put his arms around her waist and buried his head against her. "They think she's going to be okay. The doctor says things look good. She had something called a transient extreme attack."

"I shouldn't have taken Lexington," Mary said. "I couldn't get back on the loop."

"Not extreme. *Ischemic*," Henry said. "Fancy word for minor stroke."

"Well, anyways, she's going to be okay. That's what matters."

"That's great," Mary held him and burned. She had a fever and it heated every part of her body. "I'm sick. Feel my head."

Jimmy pulled away from her and gave her a curious look. Henry looked up at her, too. "Jesus, Mary," Henry said. "Can you forget about yourself for just this once?"

Mary looked at the mother, at the lump of her stomach that pushed up under the covers. The mother's eyes were closed but her mouth opened a little and she smiled.

"Maybe I should come back later," Mary said. "I think I just need some sleep and I can come in the morning." She leaned in close to Jimmy and put her hand in the middle of his chest and rubbed her palm over the front of his shirt. He was sweating and his shirt stuck to his skin.

"What if something happens?" Jimmy asked. His voice was loud, a whine, and Mary closed her eyes and stepped back. There was another bed in the room, with a pale blue curtain around it, and when Mary fell against it the metal rings that hung the fabric rattled.

"Then you can call me," she said.

"Come on. What do I have to say to make you stay?"

Mary looked over Jimmy's shoulder at Henry, who had turned to look out the window. The blinds were slanted up and a pale light from the parking lot lamps made Henry's skin look blue. Mary turned and went out the door and into the hall and Jimmy followed her. She didn't turn, but she could hear his footsteps, the slap of his flip flops, against the linoleum. She stopped at the end of the hall, in front of the elevator, and waited for him. Someone had left an empty Coke can on the floor near the elevator doors and Mary kicked it and it barreled away from her, leaving a trail of dark drops. Jimmy stood behind her and she could feel his breath brush the back of her neck when he exhaled.

"You're selfish," he said. "She's killing me. You're killing me."

Mary turned to look at him, and when she did, she lost her balance and fell back against the wall. "You said she's going to be fine. Nobody's killing you."

Jimmy put his arm against the wall, next to the side of her head, and stared down at her. His blond hair had clumped together from the sweat and his scalp blazed red underneath. He leaned in. His lips grew tight and a cluster of white lines spread around the edge of his lower lip. When he spoke, his voice was louder than Mary expected and she tried to move away from the wall, but he held his hand up and she stayed. "*You* are." He dropped his gaze and slid his hand down the wall, past Mary's shoulder. "I try to do everything for you both. I do the best I can, don't I?"

"I know you do."

"I try to take care of you and I do everything you want me to. But she's sick, right? She's in there and I don't see why it's asking too much for you to just stay. Just this once, okay?" He pulled his hand away from the wall and stepped back. "I feel like someone has opened up my head and they have their fingers in there squeezing. That's the way I feel."

Mary felt that way, too. Her face burned and her feet felt a little numb. She thought about the cool green grass in the outfield at the ballpark, the still moments of anticipation when a player walked up to the plate. "I'll come back in the morning. I'll bring clothes and coffee." She tried to put her hand to the side of his face but he stepped back, hands held up as if to push her away.

"Fine," Jimmy said. "Do what you want." Then he made a fist and hit the wall behind her, next to her head. The hit made a dull thud, like a rock falling in grass, and when he winced, Mary reached out for his arm.

"Here," she said, "let me take a look."

"Don't," he said. "Leave me alone."

"Don't leave you alone? Okay, I won't. Let me look."

Jimmy didn't laugh at her joke, which was their joke, an old one. Instead, he turned his head to look back down the hall. "Do whatever the hell you want, okay?" He paused. "I wasn't going to hit you."

"I know."

"Guess you know everything, right?"

When Mary said that she didn't, Jimmy stepped back and Mary stared past him, down the hall. The whiteness of everything hurt her eyes. When the elevator opened, Mary stepped in and, because she felt guilty, she lifted her hand and waved. She tried to smile, but Jimmy turned and the doors closed and Mary stood alone, sweating.

She drove home without looking at the directions. Her eyes oozed enough that the streetlights blurred, and she had cramps. She hadn't felt this bad since she'd gotten food poisoning in Mexico the year before when Jimmy had taken her to Cancun for her birthday. She tried to remember what she'd eaten in the last two days, what Jimmy's uncle had fed her at the restaurant, all the messed up orders he'd forced upon her while she took her breaks. He was always making her taste something, making her eat. Mary couldn't remember things clearly and she started to imagine that Jimmy was poisoning her. Mary thought of rat poison, insecticides, pills and powders with skulls on the bottle like in the cartoons. When the mouse wants to kill the cat, he goes for the bottle with the skull and crossbones, which is always there on the shelf, next to the blue and yellow bottle marked "cough syrup." Mary thought of Jimmy's mother, and the tubes, the little smile playing at the edge of her mouth when Mary walked out of the room.

Mary stayed in bed for three days and Jimmy stayed at the hospital playing canasta with his mother. At night, he would come home and make loud noises in the kitchen. He would open the refrigerator and move things around: bottles, plastic bags of ice, glass dishes filled with takeout orders from Henry's. Mary would hear the microwave hum and then Jimmy would come and stand in the doorway of the bedroom, his shoulders slumped, head tilted. Mary would pretend to sleep.

"You okay?" he'd say. "Need anything?"

Mary would sit up and rub her eyes. He would bring her water or sometimes juice if he'd just stopped downstairs and had bought some.

On his first trip home from the hospital, Jimmy told her that his mother had asked him to move into her house to take care of her. He wanted to know if Mary would come, too. He wanted Mary to marry him because his mother was Catholic and it was killing her that they were living in sin together.

"I know she's going to be okay," Jimmy said. "I know that. But what about next time? What happens next time when she's all alone?"

Mary kept quiet and stayed under the covers, sweating. She thought about the mother's flat, brown ranch house. Everything about the house was brown: the walls, the carpets, the cabinets. It was a depressing house, filled with pictures of Jesus and the Virgin Mary. Dried and rotting palms blessed every doorway.

"Just think about it," Jimmy said. "We can talk about it when you're feeling better."

Jimmy came back the second day and asked her again to marry him, and Mary thought of Jimmy's fist against the wall and she kept quiet and drank her juice. Her head felt too big for her body and her fingers were swollen. Jimmy held her hands between both of his and rubbed gently, something he sometimes did that Mary loved the feel of.

Two weeks after the mother returned home, Jimmy came home from work and filled the bathtub with water to soak the puffy taco suit. While the foam soaked, he followed Mary around the apartment, roping his arms around her waist and kissing her cheek. His hands smelled like dishwashing detergent.

"Let's take a week off and go to Padre," he said. "Let's drink margaritas and watch the sunset."

Mary thought of spring breaks in high school when she'd go to Padre with her boyfriend and the rest of the football players. She remembered bathtubs full of ice water and bottles of beer. She remembered sunburns and a cut toe from a broken bottle on the beach, boys with *bikini inspector* scripted on their tee shirts.

"No thanks," she said. Mary imagined a beach full of young ballplayers, boys with muscles and hate in their eyes. Boys that would laugh at her thighs and Jimmy's white stomach. Mary's stomach throbbed and she realized that she once belonged there, with the teenagers who were solid and angry and ready for spring. But that was fifteen years ago.

"Why not?"

"It's a place for high school jocks and cheerleaders."

"No it's not."

"Yes it is."

Jimmy poked the taco suit around in the tub with the toilet plunger. He sat on the edge and stared into the cloudy water. "Maybe I should tell Henry to find another Puffy Taco for next season," Jimmy said. "This is killing me. Waiting tables is killing me."

Mary thought of a life without the smell of Henry's in their hair, on their skin. She caught a glimpse of Jimmy in a business suit and crisp white shirt, about to leave for his job in one of the office buildings that had sprung up behind the river walk in the past year, the windows boasting slick gold tinting. "Maybe you could do something with computers," she said, before she could stop herself. "Maybe we should look into classes at Navarro again." Then she remembered the nurses at the hospital, and the cheery pink scrubs they'd worn. "I could go into nursing," she added. She saw the two of them walking out of this bathroom together, out of this apartment, into separate cars with glossy red paint and dark windows, with air conditioning cold enough that Mary got chills.

She looked up, expectant, surprised when Jimmy gave her the curious look like at the hospital before he punched the wall and a muscle in his jaw started to pulse. "I'm serious, Mary." He turned away from her and went back to stirring the taco suit, an oily halo ringing the surface of the water.

"I am being serious." Mary thought of the exact streets she would drive the next morning to get to the college admissions office, the familiar lot where they would park the car.

"I want us to get married. We can move in with Mom and we could take care of her."

Mary's image of Jimmy in a suit and tie went away and she saw the two of them, still dressed in their Henry's uniforms, sitting on the couch at Henry's mother's house. She heard the mother yell, and she saw Jimmy cry. The mother always made him cry and that's the soundtrack their life would play out against.

"I won't," Mary said.

"Won't what?" Jimmy turned and some of the water from the bathtub splashed onto the floor.

"I can't do this anymore," she said.

"Do what?"

"It can't be you and me and her."

"It's not."

"It is."

Mary stood and walked out of the room and went down the hall and to the kitchen. When she stepped outside, the hot air sucked at her skin and Mary took short, shallow breaths. She stood on the wooden platform in front of their front door and stared out over the parking lot, to the highway. She thought of getting in the car and driving away, for a week or maybe a month. She could just drive. The pain in her stomach settled for the first time in a week and she took a deep breath and held it. Jimmy opened the door and stepped behind her and wrapped his arms around her waist, and Mary felt his breath against the side of her face as she exhaled and the pain in her stomach returned. He smelled like soap, and grease, and she knew he wouldn't go with her if she asked him to. He would stay here, in the apartment, until eventually his mother would have her way and he'd pack up his taco suit, his closet full of cargo shorts and T-shirts, and he'd move into the same bedroom at his mother's house that he'd lived in when Mary had first met him. Jimmy had his mother, and Henry, and a restaurant full of cousins whose names Mary had a hard time remembering.

"Let's just talk about this later," Jimmy said. "We can get through the summer and then we'll start making plans, right? Let's just take this one step at a time."

Mary let her head fall back against Jimmy's chest and she felt the heat of him against her back and she closed her eyes and listened to the sounds of the cars pulling out of the parking lot below her.

Mary lingered in the locker room, opening up different lockers and staring at the car keys, the tennis shoes and jeans of the players until the trainer walked by and asked if she thought she should be looking through other people's stuff. Jimmy was stuck in front of the door to the locker room, getting his picture taken and posing with kids. Mary waited until the trainer went out into the dugout and then she opened another player's locker. There was a pair of khaki pants bunched up at the bottom and a T-shirt on the shelf. There was a comb, a bottle of aftershave, some Prell shampoo. A blue toothbrush with yellowing bristles. Mary caught a glimpse of the life of this player, of where he would go and what he had to look forward to. Maybe he would catch a break and move up soon, to AA or maybe even a major league contract with the Dodgers. Mary took the toothbrush and slipped it into her pocket and let it fall down against her thigh.

Jimmy came into the room and the two of them went through the dugout and onto the field. Jimmy said nothing to her; he walked in front of her with his arms held out at his sides. He was slumped forward a little, tilted as if he were about to fall forward. Mary went to help him and he pulled back from her.

"What's wrong?" Mary asked. "What's the matter?"

"Just leave me alone." His voice was low, a thick command through the mesh. "It's a bad night."

"And that's my fault?" Mary realized that is what he thought. That she was responsible for his mother, his job, his bad apartment and hangovers.

"I didn't say that," he said. "Why does it have to be anyone's fault?"

The kid at first base was a girl, small with blonde hair in two ponytails poking out of the bottom of the batting helmet that sat crooked on her head. Jimmy went straight to second base, his body still tilted forward. Mary noticed that Jimmy was wearing a pair of tennis shoes now and not the brown slip-ons that matched his tights. The tennis shoes were white and new, barely stained from the red dirt of the field, and she wondered when he had bought them.

The whistle blew and Jimmy came to her in a frenzy. His arms were pulling at the bottom of the taco suit so that he could move his legs farther apart to run faster. His head was down and Mary couldn't see his eyes through the mesh of the screen. The girl was just now getting to second base and Jimmy was going too fast. The girl wouldn't catch him. Mary pushed her hands out in front of her to get Jimmy to slow but he wasn't looking at her, and when he didn't slow down, when he seemed to be rushing right for her to knock her down to the ground, Mary decided to turn and walk away, back to the dugout. She stepped around two players who were squatted down, catching balls for the two pitchers who were warming up their arms.

When she got to the door of the dugout, Mary turned back to the field and saw that Jimmy had stopped at third base. He was turned to her, one arm up over his head, waving. Mary stood and waited for Jimmy to drop his arm but he continued to hold it up, over his head. Then he turned and looked at the child, who had stopped running and now stood halfway between second base and third. The girl stared at Jimmy, waiting for him to move like he was supposed to. Her batting helmet had come off and her blonde hair was glowing. She held her arms at her sides, her hands balled into little fists.

Leaving

If you were outside her kitchen window right now, this is what you might see: a half-lopsided sill with circular white cakes of bird shit overlaying chipped brown paint, a blue checked gingham curtain with the seam at the bottom falling loose, cheap china plates with painted daisies (two of them) in the drying rack next to the sink. And this: a man with no leg humping a woman with wet hair on top of an antique table. She's staring at the water stains on the ceiling and thinking what this might look like to someone standing outside. His left leg on the ground and the stump balanced on the edge. Her legs over the side of the table, wrapped around his waist, hooked together at the ankles. Her robe spread beneath her, still damp. She slides against the table. It's been recently waxed and buffed—only yesterday, in fact. Can you see the carved legs? The intricate spirals carved in dark mahogany? It's the most beautiful thing she owns. Take your eyes away from the stump and have a look. It's worth a fortune. She's thinking of the grooves right now, the way they twist into the wood like carved bracelets on skin. The worn-smooth ridges shiny with oil, the small feet that turn out and hook up at the ends. The curve of them more delicate than the shape of her calves.

Kate's been thinking of leaving Ryan for almost two years now. And just yesterday, while scrubbing the kitchen floor with a harsh detergent that stung her eyes, did she take the idea seriously. It's difficult leaving a man with one leg. She's had to convince herself that it's not such a terrible thing to do, that women must do it all the time. That really, when you think about it, she's just a wife leaving a husband. Things would be easier if she had a real reason, what her mother would call *concrete*. Something that could hold up in court. If he'd cheated on her, beat her up. If he'd killed her dog and buried it in the backyard, under one of the Mulberry bushes that never gets enough nutrients, anyway. But she's had to make herself realize that it's the stump. She can't stand the feel of it between her thighs anymore, the touch of scar tissue on her stomach. The way it fits so smoothly into the prosthetic leg he keeps on the floor under the bed. She thinks of this leg when she sleeps, of the caramel color and the cool plastic shine to it. She imagines it moving around their house at night, knocking into the lamp in the hall, the plant stand in the den. She refuses to unstrap it the way she used to when they'd undress. She used to enjoy this removal—how she could take her husband's leg away and stow it under the bed where they slept. She'd finger the hinges, rub her palm in the smooth curvature of the indention, still warm from his skin. The freedom excited her. She's not amazed by the idea of it anymore, though. She thinks this maybe makes her a bad person.

Ryan pushes himself off his wife and holds onto the corner of the table for balance. He hops to one side to let her up. She leans up on one elbow and pulls the robe over her lap.

"Can you get me some water?"

Ryan looks around the room for his crutch, forgetting that he left it in the hallway. He hops on one leg over to the sink.

"The water line to the ice-maker went kaput. No ice okay?" he asks her.

"That's fine." She looks at the clock. It's almost ten. Before Ryan came home, Kate pulled the suitcases from the attic and stored them in the closet in the front hallway. They smelled like mothballs and gym clothes. She left them open in the hall for over an hour, wondering how much she could fit, what she'd be able to take and what she'd have to leave behind. She'd take her mother's satin robe, of course, and the china doll she's had since she was a child. But the thought of actually taking these items and moving them to the suitcase gave her sharp pains in the stomach and she had to sit down and think things out. She decided to write a letter to Ryan while she sat on the checkered couch in the living room. It started this way: *Ryan, it's not you, it's me. I thought I could do this, but I can't anymore. I can't stand being here, in this house, with all of this mess.* She wanted to tell him more, but her head started to hurt and she couldn't put what she wanted to say in the right words. She didn't want this to be a big deal. They are, both of them, quiet people.

Ryan fills a glass with water and turns to her. Kate sits up and ties her robe.

"No, sit back, Kate. I'll bring it to you." He moves forward and loses his balance, has to drop the glass to keep himself from falling. The glass hits the floor and shatters. The sound is loud and both of them stare at the floor for several seconds, wondering what has just happened. Finally, when Kate bends down to pick up one of the larger pieces of glass, the smooth edge slices cleanly into the flesh of her finger. When she looks down, there's blood starting to form in a thin line. They both stare.

"I'm sorry," he says. "It's the floor. What did you wax it with? Oil?"

"It's not the floor." Kate slides to the other end of the table and stands up. "Leave the glass. I'll get it in the morning." She steps around the pieces of glass, glittering like earrings in the overhead light, and walks out of the room and stands in the hallway. Ryan's crutch is on the floor in front of her, the scotch tape wrapped around the bottom colored in red felt tip marker. She wants to step over it and leave; she wants to slam doors. She wants to write this moment down in the letter to Ryan. This is what she'd write: *I want to leave you because I can't slam a door after we've fought. I can't just hurt your feelings. I have to consider your body, your stump.*

She didn't always feel this way about her husband's body. At first it was a mystery, a secret she discovered in the dark.

The first night Kate met Ryan she was drunk at a bar. She was there alone. She would've looked like any other woman you'd see at that kind of bar: dyed hair too yellow, clothes a little tight, red lipstick glossed on her lips. She was there for a quick pick up, a good time. A few free drinks, the frozen kind made with thick strawberry syrup and a cherry on top, next to a paper umbrella. Those things can get expensive when you drink them all night. She had on these amazing gold snake earrings with sparkling eyes. They went down the sides of her neck and touched the straps of her tank top. She loved the sound of them when she moved on her barstool, or when she pushed her hand through her hair and shook her head to laugh. She felt all right with rum. Ryan didn't get there until the end of the night, when she'd had a lot to drink and was about to go home. He moved up behind her at the bar and she saw his face in the mirror across from them, behind the confetti-colored bottles of liquor against the back wall. His hair was long and crazy, the way she liked.

"Get you another?" he asked. He was drunk, too. From beer and a little scotch his buddy kept in a flask in his pocket. Ryan wasn't that used to drinking. She thought the limp was from the liquor.

She liked the size of his hands, the way the hairs grew wiry on top of them.

She went back to his house and maneuvered him into the bedroom. She pulled his shirt over his head, felt her way along his arms. She undid the buttons on his jeans and he flinched a little, then pulled away from her and groaned.

"What's wrong?" she asked him. "Isn't this what you want?"

She knelt in front of him and pulled down the jeans, looking up at his face. When she felt the plastic she stopped. He pulled back and she moved in closer, inspecting the plastic calf she held in her hands. He reached down and touched her hair, was about to say something soothing. To offer an explanation, or a joke. But before he could she laughed a little, then couldn't stop. She leaned back on the floor and laughed and covered her face and cried a little. He watched her wipe her eyes on the tank top she pulled up from her jeans.

"I'll take you home," he said.

"No," she told him. "I want to stay."

He moved on top of her and she felt the emptiness between her legs. She moved her arm down and touched the place where his leg cut off, right above where his knee would have been. The skin was tight and smooth, like plastic Saran wrap. Or a shower curtain. Only the texture was rough in places, like the plastic had melted. She couldn't stop touching him. Couldn't stop the excitement she felt from touching something so unnatural for the first time. The excitement of touching a part of someone else and not feeling skin, her fingers unable to press indentations.

In the morning, she stayed and made him breakfast—fried eggs and pancakes. She turned and saw him in the doorway. He was naked. His crutch was cradled in the crook of his arm and he looked beautiful in the light. Like a marble statue at the museum, where the leg has crumbled away but the rest of the body is perfectly carved. They ate breakfast together, naked, at the drafting table he had set up in the corner of the kitchen.

"I'll need a real table," she said to him. "Something sturdy."

"I'll get you whatever you want."

She liked the way he steadied his arms on the table, between the plates.

Ryan follows Kate into the bedroom and turns on the television. Professional wrestling, which is what he watches every night before he goes to bed. This is his nightly ritual. It starts with the wrestling, then fifty push-ups on the floor by the bed. Then he showers with shave gel to soften his skin. He falls asleep after that, with a damp towel still wrapped around his waist.

Even the sex in the kitchen—he's incorporated that into his nightly routine. He waits until she's out of the shower. He takes her, always, on the table these days, as if he can't imagine messing up the sheets before going to sleep.

Kate sits in a chair in the corner of the room and watches him. The reflection from the television shines in his eyes, miniature men moving each other around. She is wondering whether she can carry the quilt on the bed with her in the morning, whether it will fit in with the satin robe and the picture albums she's decided to take. The quilt is a beautiful wedding ring design, with deep burgundy stitching. Her mother gave it to them as a wedding present. She had it sent to them through the mail, with a card. Kate wasn't upset that her mother didn't come to their wedding. They hadn't planned well. The ceremony was a spontaneous thing, down at city hall on a Thursday afternoon. She'd worn a rented dress with a small tear at the waist. Ryan had worn a tuxedo borrowed from his brother. They stayed home for a honeymoon, painting the front porch a robin's egg blue.

Things she wants to take but can't: the dresser with the gold painted flowers on the drawers, the soft Persian rug with the deep red oriental design, the china clock with the hand- painted Roman numerals on the face.

Kate walks into the bathroom and opens the medicine cabinet. Her necessities are here. Aspirin, tweezers, a comb. She separates her items from Ryan's, placing them on different shelves. She knows he won't notice this move, this small manipulation. She wonders whether he'll think back after she's gone and remember this gesture. Remember reaching to the top shelf for his deodorant and finding it moved to the bottom, with his witch hazel. She doesn't think he will. He's not one to notice such small events. She moves his electric razor and a hair falls from the blade onto the white porcelain counter. She takes a piece of toilet paper and pushes the hair into the sink. It's surprisingly long and thick. She rinses out the sink until the hair is gone.

She opens the linen closet and searches through the towels, the sets of sheets. These are things she may need. She doesn't know where she'll go. Her friends are Ryan's. If she went to one of them, they'd let him know. She wants this break to be clean. She wants to go away and not have to say his name to anyone. She knows that if she says his name enough she'll need to come back. She'll miss his routine and the sound of his voice. She's afraid, also, of what the friends will think of her. She's afraid they'll look at her and know why she left. They'll say to each other behind her back that she's a horrible person, to leave someone because of his body. And she'll have to agree with them. But what can she say? How can she describe what it's like to not want the feel of something against your body? To want to look away?

Kate takes a set of sheets from the closet and sets them on the counter by the sink. They're her favorite set. Flannel white sheets with little blue butterflies. She carries them into the bedroom.

Ryan is on the ground doing his push-ups. The leg is on. Sweat drips down the stump and into the crevice where the leg fits on. Kate looks away.

"Do you like these sheets?" she asks him.

Ryan pauses and looks up. "Not really, why?"

"Just thinking of throwing them away." She sits on the edge of the bed and watches him do more push-ups. "Would you miss them if I threw them out?"

"Do what you want." Ryan's face is red. He collapses onto the ground and spreads out his arms. "Get me a towel, will you?"

Kate walks into the bathroom and takes a towel from the hook on the back of the door and then walks back into the bedroom and hands it to him. Ryan sits up and wipes off his face. He reaches down to take off the leg but his hands are wet and they slip.

He looks up at Kate. "Could you give me a hand?"

Kate bends down and wraps her hands around the hard ankle. When Ryan leans back, she pulls the leg toward her chest. The prosthetic pulls off easily and she holds it against her, the weight of it causing her to sit back against the side of the bed. Ryan wipes the stump with the towel and Kate looks down at the leg she holds. She's come to think of this leg as a part of him and it hurts her to hold it this way now, detached. Dead weight. He doesn't think about it as a part of him, he never has. It's a tool, a piece of equipment. Something to even him out. Back when she found this removal erotic, she'd take her time and touch each scratch in the plastic. Ryan would move her hands to his chest, his crotch, but she'd move away and go back to the leg. It fascinated her. The fact that she could take a part of him and move away with it. To another room, another town. When she understood that, to Ryan, it was something easily replaced, a molded piece of plastics and rubber, the leg lost its appeal for her. She began to see it as an imposter, a fake. Something to store under the bed. Her husband had no ritual for removing the leg. It was something to be pulled off, wiped, left on the floor.

Ryan goes into the bathroom and shuts the door. She hears the shower go on and the curtain being pulled back. She thinks of him under the water, leaning against the blue tiles. She imagines him touching himself, getting excited, but she knows this is just her imagination. She knows him better than that. This is what she understands: when she married him she believed it exciting to be with a man with one leg. They could be careless, ready for anything. He would do things that would always surprise her. But she knows what he's doing right now by the sounds she hears from the other room. He would never do anything to embarrass her.

Kate goes into the hallway and opens the closet where the suitcases are stacked on top of each other. She wants to be ready to go before he wakes up. She knows he'll go to work, anyway. He won't try to find her until after, and by that time she will be in another state. She can have everything packed by four, she thinks. If he doesn't hear her pulling things from the drawers. She should have packed her clothes during the day, but she worried about the smell from the suitcases. She didn't want to take that smell with her, that scent of decay. She takes down the picture albums from the top shelf of the closet and puts them at the bottom of the suitcase. These are pictures of her from before she met Ryan, when she was younger and not settled. When she wore her hair in a difficult braid down her back. She's become simpler since being with him; he's taught her the benefits of efficiency.

Kate hears the shower go off in the other room and she shuts the door to the closet. When she returns to the bedroom, she sees him on the bed with the towel around his waist. He's on top of the quilt, water dripping onto it and leaving dark circles. She decides the quilt will have to stay. Ryan closes his eyes and holds his arm across her side of the bed.

"Are you coming to bed?" he asks. "I could use a shoulder rub."

"I'm going to clean up some first."

Ryan opens his eyes and stares at her. "Is something wrong?"

Kate walks to the edge of the bed and stares down at Ryan. His skin is flushed from the shower, bright red on his arms, his neck. "Why? Is anything wrong with you?"

"No," he says.

"What would be wrong with me?"

"Just asking." He closes his eyes again and puts one arm over his face. "Shut off the light on the way out, will you?"

Kate leans over him and stretches to reach the quilt underneath him. She tugs to get it out from under him.

"Leave it off," he says, irritated. "I'm hot as hell."

"I want to wash it." Kate tugs again.

"Tonight?" He groans. "Just leave it. You can do it in the morning."

Kate lets go of the quilt and continues to stare. The stump is resting easily against one of the rings. Water beads up at the end of it, over the marbleized tissue, and rolls onto the quilt. She feels a tightness in her stomach, like she's going to be sick. "Fine," she says. She's decided she'll never get this image out of her head, anyway. He can keep the quilt. She'll get another.

Kate fell in love with Ryan on the day he brought her the table. They'd been living together for awhile. She was home washing dishes, staring out to the backyard where the birds sat side by side on top of the low concrete wall that bordered the edge of the yard. Her dog was asleep in the center of the yard. She heard Ryan's truck pull up in the driveway and she turned off the water. They were at the point in their relationship where they met each other with anticipation. He would come home surprised that she was still there, in the kitchen, or the bedroom, maybe. Waiting for him. She waited for the day he would come home and ask her to leave. She'd been with men before and had come to expect this. They were at that point where things could go that way.

She opened the door off the kitchen and saw his truck and something in the back, covered with a blanket. He came around the side and waved her over.

"Come take a look," he said.

Kate walked to the bed of the truck and peered under the blanket. She saw the carvings in the legs of the table and she ran her hands down the grooves, slid her fingers into the spirals.

"It cost me a fortune, so I hope it's what you like."

They moved it into the house and Kate spent the next hour waxing the top until it was smooth and shiny. She cleaned the carved spirals with Q-tips dipped in polish. Ryan sat at one of the chairs and watched her under the table, feeling the legs. She moved over to where he was and pulled the edge of his sweatpants over his plastic leg. She took the polish and wiped, believing, as she did with the table, that if she cleaned it enough, she could make it her own. Ryan lifted her up and put her on top of the table. He lifted her skirt and felt the inside of her thighs, the smooth skin cool to his touch. When she felt him inside her, she reached under and held the leg of the table. Its sturdiness comforted her. She felt a connection between this table and what they were doing. The wood was dark and soft, would give under the pressure of her thumbnail.

Ryan sat with her at the table later that night, after she'd set two places with chipped plates and a vase of flowers. She served him spaghetti and he asked her to get married.

"Nothing fancy," he'd said. "Just the two of us."

She felt a comfort in the room and said yes. She believed she had everything she could want. He seemed to know what she needed and gave it to her.

Kate goes into the kitchen and gets the broom. She sweeps up the pieces of glass, which are scattered like pebbles on the floor. She steps around the pieces carefully, sweeping them into the dustpan and making trips to the trashcan to dump them away. Still, after she's finished sweeping the floor, she imagines there are tiny slivers of glass still under her feet. She takes a dishtowel and gets on the floor, under the table. She wipes the floor in a circular motion. Her arm moves mechanically, her eyes fixed on the checkered linoleum. She runs her palm against the surface, feeling for pieces of glass. The floor feels slick and clean, but she doesn't trust her sense of touch. She stands and walks over to the cabinet under the kitchen sink and takes out the basket of cleaning supplies. She squirts wax on the floor and starts to rub it in. It hazes over and then she rubs again to make the linoleum shine. She does this in small sections, starting at the area by the sink. She keeps her eyes focused on the floor. When she finishes this, she starts again at the sink and repeats the process. After the second coat, she crawls under the table and curls her legs to her chest. She sleeps against the smooth floor, forgetting about the suitcase in the hall closet, the quilt on the bed.

Exactly two months after their wedding, Kate felt her separation from Ryan begin. They were in the bedroom; she was undressing him. She had pulled off his jeans and he was on the bed watching her feel the leg. She had her fingers wrapped around the ankle. She moved her hand down to the smooth foot. She touched the creases which served as toes. She reached over and wrapped her arms around the leg and smelled the plastic. Ryan exhaled.

"You know," he said. "I can't feel a thing when you touch it."

"I like the way it feels. It's part of you."

Ryan reached out and unwrapped her hands from the leg. "It's not a part of me. It's a piece of plastic."

He reached down and took off the leg and held it in his hands. "It's comes off and slides under the bed."

Kate reached out and held the leg. "I want you to leave it on." She moved to put it back on and he stopped her.

"I'm not keeping it on. It's just going to get in the way."

"Put it back on or I won't sleep with you." Kate was on her knees, holding the ankle.

"Fine," he said. "Sleep with *it*, then. I'm going to bed."

Ryan got up from the bed and carried a pillow to the living room and slept on the checkered couch. Kate lay in bed, awake, her hand on the plastic leg which was next to her on the bed. She left her hand, balled in a fist, in the crevice where his stump would fit.

Ryan moves around the kitchen in the morning, making coffee and pancakes. Kate stays curled under the table, pretending to sleep, until the coffee is ready. When she sits up, she hits her head hard on the edge of the table and Ryan laughs. She stares up at him, her face burning. Kate's sure that Ryan was not surprised to walk into the kitchen and find her asleep on the floor. She does this sometimes, when she has something on her mind, or when she can't sleep, and he's gotten used to this. He knows she's always there, curled in a corner, under the table she loves. He leaves her alone.

Kate watches Ryan move from the refrigerator to the stove. He pours her a cup of coffee and leaves it on the counter. Kate comes out from under the table and goes to the counter for the mug. Her head is congested and her back is sore. The cut on her arm is closed, a stain of blood in the crevice of the cut. Her robe falls open and she is naked underneath. She leaves it open and goes to sit at the table. She believes he dropped the glass on purpose, to make her stay. He knows that if she leaves him it will have to be at night, when there are no clothes stacked in the laundry room, or dishes in the sink. There are too many distractions for her during the day.

"Sleep okay?" he asks her.

"Fine." She takes a sip of the coffee and lets him pour the syrup over her pancakes. She thinks about what she'll do for the rest of the day: wash the quilt, fold her clothes, bathe the dog. She'll try to pack the suitcases while he's away. She won't think about the pain of removing these items scattered around the house. She eats her breakfast with her robe left open, and crumbs of food fall onto her stomach and stick to the light layer of sweat on her skin. Ryan eats his breakfast across from her, staring out the window to the side of her head. When he finishes, he leaves his dishes on the table and stands to leave.

"See you tonight?" he asks.

"I'll make fettuccini," she says. "With the garlic bread and the spread you like."

"Sounds good." He kisses the top of her head and leaves.

Maybe tonight, she thinks.

She watches him limp down the sidewalk to his truck and she remembers the suitcases, the quilt, the clock. She's about to turn away from Ryan because she doesn't think she can stand to watch him climb into his truck, but then he stops walking and pauses, briefly, to pat the top of the dog's head. He puts his hand gently between the dog's ears and rubs, and she likes the way they look together, in the sunlight, both of them connected before he pulls his hand away and continues down the path to the driveway. He pauses at the gate to wave back at her but she has already turned her attention to the mess of crumbs on the table, which she brushes with the tips of her fingers into a small pile.

If you were outside her kitchen window right now, staring in through the thick glass and mesh screen, this is what you might see: a woman, half-naked, robe untied and slipping off her shoulder. Take your eyes away from her body, her breasts. Look at the table. At the carved legs, at how beautiful they look in the sun.

The way the light catches the shine to show every scratch, each imperfection.

Krum, Texas

Sheila's new neighbor sat in her driveway, in his wheelchair, and from where she stared at him (through her kitchen window, the small one over the sink) it looked as if he had the front of his pants open, touching himself. It was hard to tell for sure because of the baggy sweatshirt he wore and so Sheila continued her stare until he looked up and caught her. At least she thought he did, but because of the reflection of sunlight off his glasses, she couldn't be sure. Then he lifted one of his hands up and waved. He shouted something that Sheila couldn't hear.

"What was that?" she yelled through the window.

The neighbor waved again. "Come out and say hi," he said. "I don't bite."

Sheila had been in this new house only a week and she'd seen this neighbor fifteen times already, maybe more. He looked about thirty, same as her, but he could have been older or younger; it was hard to tell with the tinted glasses he wore and the distance he usually kept. He seemed to always wear the same black sweatshirt with a giant guitar shaped like a skull plastered on the front—an ancient heavy metal band logo Sheila vaguely recognized—faded jeans with holes at the knees, and padded leather gloves with openings notched out at the knuckles. His wheelchair, covered with bright and peeling stickers, was motorized; she could hear the small engine hum up and down the sidewalk in front of her house, sometimes as late as two in the morning.

"What's that?" she yelled again. Then, before the neighbor could answer, Sheila went to the front hallway. From the narrow window next to the door she could see him, still parked and staring at the kitchen window. She opened the front door and walked onto the porch. Beneath her bare feet, the wood planks groaned.

"Over here," she yelled.

The neighbor turned his head and nodded. His black hair looked electric, a comic halo of exclamation points, and his eyes, beneath his glasses, appeared thumbed with charcoal. When the neighbor pushed at something on the arm of the chair he started to move forward, then rolled back. He was stuck in the gravel. He tried again, rolled back again, then hit his fist on the arm of the wheelchair. "Shit," he said. Then he said it two more times.

Sheila stood on the porch and watched until the neighbor maneuvered up the front walkway. From her porch, which was raised, she could see that he'd pushed his sweatshirt down over his lap. He stopped at the foot of the stairs to her porch and looked up at her.

"You should pave that driveway," he said. His speech was deliberate, like a first grader having a difficult time sounding out particular vowels. Sheila watched as he folded his hands in his lap. His legs were amazingly thin, anorexic or cancer-thin, and close-up the neighbor looked older. Thirty-five, maybe. His hair was long, past his shoulders, and feathered back on both sides. A little gray had sprung up at the temples. He reached down, into a pouch that hung off the left side of his wheelchair, and pulled out a plastic comb. It was the kind Sheila used to carry in the back pocket of her jeans when she was in junior high, with a big curved handle and large plastic teeth. Instead of brushing it through his hair, though, he held it there, in his lap. He curved his fingers around the handle. "I live right next to you," he said, "with my mother."

Sheila went to the second step and sat in front of him. She was about to ask if she should get used to him hanging out in front of her house, masturbating, but the way he'd said *mother*, so careful and quiet, stopped her.

"I know," she said, although she didn't. She knew that he lived in the house next door because she had seen him go down the ramp on the side of the house on the day she moved in, but she hadn't yet seen anyone else come out of the house.

"I'm Mark." He held out his hand and Sheila took it carefully. His palm was warm and moist and she pulled away too quickly but he held it out and waited for her to take it again. "Go on," he said. "Shake it like you mean it." Sheila reached out but Mark pulled his hand away before she could take hold, his fingertips lightly grazing hers. He laughed—a deep sound that seemed more like a cough. "Got you," he said. "Didn't see that one coming, did you?" Sheila noticed that one side of his face pulled up in a grimace when he smiled while the skin on the other side avalanched to the chin. He closed both his eyes and tilted back his head. "Bet you're wondering why I'm in the chair."

"Not really," Sheila said. She concentrated on the tiny walnut of an Adam's apple that punctuated the whiskered skin of his neck. "I mean, you don't have to say anything if you don't want to."

He smiled; he wore braces on his lower teeth and the wires glittered dully in the late morning sun. "Wrecked my car in high school. Had this badass 280ZX and I flipped it going eighty. Killed my girlfriend."

"Oh my God," Sheila said. She touched her fingers to her lips.

"Just kidding," he said. "No, really. Just about the girlfriend. The rest is the truth, though. My brain was like back and forth, you know? Like it actually moved around in my skull. That's why I talk slow. I'm not stupid, though. I'm not messed up like a lot of people think. I went back and got my GED, right?" His hands shook. Every few seconds his fingers would twitch and he'd grip the handle of his plastic comb tighter. Then he turned his head away and stared hard at his own house, down the road. "You could be my girlfriend," he said quietly.

"Sorry?" Sheila said. She felt her chest get hot, the side of her neck begin to tingle, and tried the breathing technique the therapist recommended. Deep breath in for the count of two, then exhale. Mark turned and stared straight at her, through the dark lenses of his glasses.

Inside her house, the phone started to ring. She could hear its whine through the front door, which had swung open. Sheila knew it was her mother, calling for her daily check-in and to tell Sheila, once again, the reasons she should have stayed in Michigan and fought her dismissal. Mark moved his head to look around Sheila, into her house.

"I guess I should get that," Sheila said. "Maybe I'll see you later."

"Okay," Mark said. "Rock and roll." He stuck his thumb up in the air at her, a gesture of optimism.

A week in Krum, Texas was enough for Sheila to know that her mother was right, that she should have waited out her suspension. It was December and snowing in Michigan when she left, but here it felt like July to her, seventy degrees and the sun close enough that it would burn your arms if you stayed outside too long. The mountain cedar blew in from the south, even in winter, and kept her nose running and her eyes swollen and red. And this house, buried on a half-acre of flat yellow grass and a small murky pond, tilted, slightly, to the left, so that when Sheila dropped a marble on her kitchen floor it rolled, almost immediately, through the front hallway and into the living room. The road to her house was a potholed mess that curved off the two-lane highway that ran straight through downtown Krum. Not that there was any real downtown, just a block of buildings: a small market, a diner, a hardware store. The school where she would teach three different grades and four different subjects was a flat stretch of cinder block near the highway, the bright graffiti covering the sides of the building written in a language of symbols Sheila couldn't decipher.

Later, a few hours after the neighbor disappeared, Sheila sat out on her front porch and drank coffee as she stared out across the farm road in front of her house and thought about what she needed from the corner market in town: milk, some cheese crackers, a six-pack of beer. The landscape of Texas confused her. The expanse in front of her house was flat enough that she could see straight through downtown Krum, past the highway and to the next county, maybe. The people drove the roads recklessly, their bumper-stickered pick-ups spotted with patches of bondo and primer. Sheila thought about the neighbor and his accident and wondered what it would have been like to grow up in this town. How would a date play out if you went to high school here? Beer drinking on top of one of the pump jacks that dotted all of the fields here, followed by a drunken ride out to the small, clotted lake at the edge of town? She imagined all sorts of horrible automobile accidents happened to teenagers in a place like this.

She sat until her coffee grew cold and then she got into her Honda with the Michigan license plates and drove down Main Street, through town. Right after she turned by the house on the corner—the one with the roof sunk in on one side and a pack of dogs circling the front porch—she gripped the wheel and a pain shot up her right arm, sharp enough that she pulled to the side of the road and put her face in her hands and let herself scream. Anxiety, her doctor had guessed before she left Michigan, although until now she hadn't felt any pain since the classroom chair had gotten thrown, a child's bone had almost been broken. She hit the dashboard with her fist and sat staring at the empty road in front of her until a pick-up truck came up beside her and a kid—a teenager—with a thin mustache leaned across the seat, rolled down his passenger window and said something to her.

He looked a little like an ex-boyfriend she had lived with once, for a few months, when she was in college. Thin face, large brown eyes set a little too close together. He'd wanted to cover the walls of their apartment with old Steve McQueen movie posters.

The teenager next to her honked his horn and then stuck his tongue out at Sheila and wiggled it obscenely. Through the dusty glass of her car window the tongue looked gray, like something dead, and Sheila had an uneasy feeling that in Krum, Texas an unattached woman was open to the first man who could muscle his way into her life and that somehow, maybe, this fate was what she deserved.

At her house, the neighbor was parked, as usual, in her driveway. He stared up at her kitchen window, perhaps expecting to see her washing the dinner dishes or making some coffee. He had his hands gripped on both wheels of his chair and he didn't turn when Sheila pulled up behind him and stopped, her passage to the garage blocked. She was slow to get out of the car. When she did, when he heard her car door slam, he turned his head around and smiled at her. Sheila held the paper bag full of groceries against her chest.

"How's things?" he asked.

"Just peachy," she said. Then Sheila realized this was a phrase of her mother's, what she said when she was annoyed and someone asked her how she was doing.

Sheila went up to her porch and Mark followed. The wheelchair hummed behind her and she turned around, finally, and waited.

"Look," she said. "I need to go inside and sleep for awhile." Sheila felt the condensation from the six-pack of beer bleed through the paper grocery sack against her chest. She thought about the boy's tongue, his anemic mustache.

Mark nodded and folded his hands. The cuffs of his black sweatshirt had started to come apart and he'd changed jeans since earlier in the day. The ones he wore now were covered with bleach stains and small tears and she could see his kneecaps, knobby and white, through the web of white threads that had come undone around the holes.

"I can understand that," he said. "I can. Sometimes all I want to do is spend all day in bed." He picked at a hole in the cuff of his sweatshirt. "The thing is, I'm gonna take you to dinner on Thursday."

The orange horizon burned around him, a curtained flame, and Sheila noticed that he slumped forward in his chair a little, from a curve in his spine, maybe, and this made her think of the line of children in the hallways at school on Scoliosis screening day, bent at the waist, fingertips touching their toes while the visiting nurse went slowly in front of them, nodding her head. The dirt around him was orange, too. Mud stuck in clumps to the tires on his chair.

"I don't think I can do that," Sheila said. "I have class prep to finish." She took a deep breath and counted to three before she let it out, then started up the stairs to go into her house. When she got to the front door she turned and gave him a little wave, after she got the key into the lock and felt it click open. She waved good-bye and he lifted his hand from his lap and pumped his fist into the air.

"Thursday," he said. "I want you to think about it." Then the fist dropped back into his lap like a deflated balloon.

Inside, she stripped off her coat, her sweater, her black wool pants. She'd accidentally left the thermostat up too high, still used to the settings she kept in Detroit, so she stood at her kitchen window in her white cotton underwear and T-shirt and watched the neighbor sit in his chair. His head was tilted to the left, his arms folded across his chest. Behind him, the sky began to bruise a deep purple. She thought about the teenager in the truck and how it would have been easy to let him follow her home. How easy it might have been to let him into her house, let him strip away her clothes and take her. On the table, in the kitchen. The way he would have held her down by her wrists until he was deep inside of her, the backs of her legs gathering bruises from the sharp metal lip that curved around the edge of the table.

She had remained silent when Principal Lawson had called her into his office after the thrown chair, which had narrowly missed Harmony Johnson, who was standing at the front chalkboard, refusing to diagram a sentence and instead yelling *fuck you, bitch* on a continual loop. The chair had hit the chalkboard only a few inches from Harmony's right arm, the pieces skittering to the far corner of the room after cracking against the board. He had kept his eyes steady on Sheila's face while he waited for an explanation, then finally mentioned her required suspension. There would have to be a little therapy, negotiated by her union rep. A month without pay. But she'd be back after the holiday. *An accident, right?* Who else would want to teach that class? All those fatherless children? But as he reviewed her teaching file, Sheila felt relief loosen her bones as she realized that she'd never have to listen to Harmony Johnson call her a bitch ever again, or any of the other string of names they'd come up with for her as they sat grouped together at their desks, angrily ignoring their textbooks.

At nine o'clock that night, Sheila woke up. Something was scratching at her front door. She could hear the scraping all the way in her bedroom, at the back of the house. She had fallen asleep naked and the house had cooled. She reached for the sweatshirt that was on the floor next to her mattress. Her fingers felt numb.

When she opened the front door, a dog went between her legs, into the house. It was a big one, black. A Labrador like the one her father had gotten her when she was a kid.

"What the fuck?" Sheila said. She pushed hard at the dog's head with her hands until it growled.

"He won't bite." Mark was in his chair, in the same place he'd been sitting the last time she looked, before she went to sleep. Sitting in his chair at the bottom of the stairs to her porch, holding his comb and smiling. The white letters and guitar on his sweatshirt glowed against the black background.

"I don't care." Sheila left the door open and walked out onto the porch and the dog followed her. He circled her, panting. "What do you want?" she asked, unable to filter her anger. "Why don't you go home?"

"I thought you'd maybe want to get a beer. I brought my van."

Sheila looked past him and saw a black van, new and shiny, parked in her driveway.

"You drive?" The words slipped out, and even through her anger Sheila was embarrassed, but Mark didn't seem to mind.

"I drive all the time," he said. "Got that van special made just for me. Hand brake and accelerator and all that."

"It's late," she said. "I was sleeping."

"Well you're up now." He shook his keys at her and the dog ran down the stairs and jumped at the sound. Mark patted the top of its head.

"Where's a bar around here?" Sheila couldn't remember seeing any bars on Main Street, or on any of the small side streets which seemed to only be cluttered with garages and body shops, the spaces in front of the buildings littered with the rusted corpses of cars.

"I know a place," he said. "Not too far away."

He waited awhile for Sheila to answer, and when she didn't, he started to turn his wheelchair around. One of the wheels slipped off the pavement and the dog went around him, wagging his tail. "Stay home if you want," he said. "Don't do me any favors." He went towards his van but stopped before he got to the driveway and turned back around to her. "I only wanted to get you out of the house for a bit," he said. "Just thought you might want to see what's around. All you do is sit in your house."

"I was *sleeping*."

"Sure. Whatever."

Sheila stood and watched as Mark pulled himself into the front seat of the van. Despite his legs, which seemed to hang straight down, like pieces of wood, his movements had grace to them. He was in the front seat in one fluid movement, then he swung his legs in front of him and stared forward, through the windshield. The chair sat empty on the ground next to him, the dog on the gravel by one of the wheels, looking up. Mark slapped his lap and the dog jumped up, crawled over him, and settled on the passenger seat.

"Look," Sheila said, "it's just late. Maybe I can get a raincheck?" Another phrase Sheila had never used before, another phrase of her mother's.

"No prob." Mark smiled and his lip curled up. His anger seemed to evaporate and hers did too. "Hey, so, dinner?"

"Thursday? Is that tomorrow?" Sheila asked. She realized that she had lost track of her days since she had moved. Her head felt thick and gauzy.

"Sure is," he said. "Hey, throw my chair in the back?"

Sheila had forgotten about the wheelchair, which had become a part of the neighbor's body in her mind, and now she turned to look at the empty chair to the side of her. Mark told her to press the release button on the side to make the chair collapse and she did. When she picked it up to put it in the seat behind Mark, the chair was lighter than she had expected.

She slammed the door and he started the van and turned the stereo on. A loud, heavy song Sheila didn't recognize blasted out through the open window. Mark nodded at her and pounded his fist on the top of the dashboard before he put the van into gear and pulled out of Sheila's driveway. She stood and watched the red taillights of the van as it curved along the edge of their road. When it disappeared, Sheila went and sat on the steps of her front porch to wait and see if he was going to come back. A wind kicked up and Sheila pulled the sweatshirt over her knees and then leaned back against the rail next to the front steps. She was glad the weather had grown cold, finally.

In the morning, she thought she should prepare for school. She would start teaching in a week and hadn't yet bothered to open the battered-looking textbooks the school had mailed to her. They sat on the kitchen counter in a neat pile, their peeling covers an omen. The book on top had a confusing picture of what looked, from this angle, like a marble shooting through the back of a man's head. She walked away from them, though, and instead stood in the back corner of the kitchen, away from the window, and prepared herself for the neighbor. Without thinking, she combed her fingers through her hair, smoothed down her shirt, then tucked it into her jeans. When she finally went and pulled back the curtains, her arm raised over her head, she found herself disappointed to see an empty yard.

She thought he might have figured out a way to wheel his chair around to the side of the house, where the owner had made a path with crushed stone, and so she went out to the front porch and looked around the side of the house. When she didn't see him there, Sheila sat on the front steps and waited. Through the bare trees at the edge of the property she could see the back of his shiny van, parked too close to the road. The sun bounced off the small bubble window, situated over the rear tire, which stuck out from the smooth side like a fish's eye.

At six that night, just as the setting sun burned through the kitchen window, Sheila parted the curtains and saw the neighbor in his chair. She had wasted the day napping, then flipping through an old issue of *People* she found in one of the kitchen cabinets. Mark was dressed in the usual jeans and sweatshirt, but he had knotted a tie around his neck and in one hand, the one he usually reserved for his comb, he carried a clump of purple flowers.

"Come on," he yelled. "I came to get you."

"Hold on," Sheila yelled back. "Wait a minute."

Outside, the air was cold and Sheila crossed her arms over her chest as she walked beside the neighbor. The hum of Mark's wheelchair made her worry about a car coming too fast around the corner and smacking them into the soggy drainage ditch buried in the tall weeds by the side of the road. She kept looking over her shoulder but Mark stared ahead. Behind the skeletal trees in front of her, Sheila got a good look at the house, finally, that she had only caught glimpses of on the day she moved in. The dark red paint had started to chip away and gray patches of old wood showed through. The front porch sagged away from the house and a row of dead plants, under the railing, lined the edge. The wooden ramp along the side of the house, though, looked new and had been painted a cheery yellow.

"You like Van Halen?" Mark asked. Sheila turned her eyes away from the ramp ahead of her and looked down at Mark.

"What?" She thought, at first, that Mark was referring to his van, which was parked at the end of the ramp, and she turned to nod her head at it. "Sure," she said. "It's great."

Mark followed her gaze and started to laugh. "Not my ride, man. I'm talking about the band. You know, Eddie Van Halen?" He shook his head and let out a slow whistle. "Saw them tour in eighty-four and I about lost my shit. That guy can *play*. I used to play, too."

"Guitar?"

"I had a band. Used to sing, and my girlfriend would lean right up against the stage the whole time we played."

"You don't play anymore?"

"Nah," he paused. "Well, sometimes."

The ramp led to a sliding glass door that opened up to a small, empty room with clean wooden floors. Mark wheeled in front of her and Sheila stared at the back of his head, at the wave of hair that had probably formed when he was sleeping. Past the empty room, the house was cramped with furniture and knickknacks, every available flat surface covered with glass vases, animal statues, small figurines of apple-cheeked children. The clutter overwhelmed her and Sheila had a hard time finding a place to focus her attention. Mark maneuvered around the furniture with grace, even when Sheila was sure his chair would bump one of the delicate tables and send the scatter of figurines perched on the surface to the floor.

She followed Mark to the dining room, which had a large front window that looked over the front lawn, onto the street. A dark table, large enough to fill the room, was already set for dinner.

"Sit," Mark said. "There's catfish and cornbread." He dropped the bunch of flowers onto the edge of the table then wheeled himself out of the room.

Sheila stood in the corner of the room and stared out the front window. The patch of dead grass in the field across the road made Sheila think of the cramped yards of the houses in her mother's neighborhood. There you could sit in your kitchen and watch your neighbor wash the dishes.

Sheila could feel Mark's mother in the room before she spoke. She could hear her slippers slide against the smooth wood, and the wheezy breathing sound she made when she moved.

"So you're the new one next door?"

Sheila turned and was surprised to see a tall woman, maybe six feet, with a shock of dyed orange hair. Behind her, she pulled an oxygen tank, new and shiny. She wore soft blue eye shadow, orange lipstick, and perfectly round circles of rouge on her cheeks. Sheila nodded at the woman and looked towards the kitchen. The matted pink bathrobe the woman wore had slipped open and Sheila could see the thin, white skin that covered the woman's chest. She could see the blue veins underneath, too, and a few bright, red bumps.

"I'm going to be teaching at the middle school," Sheila said.

"What?" The woman said. She seemed angry. "In the middle of the year you're going to start?"

"Well, there was a woman who went on maternity leave," Sheila said. "I'm going to fill in for her."

The mother narrowed her eyes and shuffled closer. She looked at the table and the purple flowers, which had started to wilt.

"So where'd he go?"

"I think he's in the kitchen," Sheila said. Sheila wondered if Mark had told his mother about the dinner. The table only had two place settings, and Sheila couldn't decide what the mother would do while they ate. Watch them? Go into another room and listen to them? The mother walked into the kitchen and the wheels of her oxygen tank squealed behind her. She had to duck her head when she stepped through the arched doorway that went into the kitchen. Sheila stepped around the table and looked in at them. Mark was leaned over a short table in the far corner of the room and his mother stood hunched over him, inspecting something over his shoulder.

"Cut the pieces larger or they'll break apart," the mother said.

Then Mark backed the chair away from her and came into the dining room, a tray of cornbread balanced on his lap. He had taken off his sunglasses and brushed his hair. There were speckles of something white on his tie.

"Grab a seat," he said. "Don't cost nothing." His mouth worked itself into a grimace and he put the tray of cornbread onto the table next to one of the plates. The pieces of bread were arranged to form a smiley face on the tray.

Sheila sat in the chair that faced the kitchen and watched as Mark wheeled food in. There was catfish, deep fried, and okra. There was corn on the cob adorned with tiny plastic swords. A layered salad with spinach, mushrooms, and what looked like arugula. He placed each dish carefully on the table, then asked her what she wanted to drink. He cupped his hands on his knees and waited for her to answer.

"Water?" Sheila guessed. The table had become so crowded with dishes that she couldn't find a place to rest her arms and so she held them crossed against her chest.

"What?" Mark shook his head. "How about wine? White or red?" he asked. "The red's in a bottle and the white is boxed stuff, so make your choice."

Sheila looked at the wine glasses on the table. Hers was smudged with a greasy thumbprint. "Red, then," she said.

The mother came into the room and sat in the other chair. She balanced the tank against the wall behind her and then pulled down a bar to lock the wheels in place. She glanced behind her, then unfolded the napkin next to her plate and put it neatly in her lap.

The mother smoothed her napkin and avoided Sheila's eyes. "Have you accepted the love of Jesus Christ?" She asked Sheila. She didn't wait for her to answer. "Because he still don't love Jesus with all his heart. All these years, even after what he done."

Sheila raised her eyes to the mother, expecting an explanation, but saw that the mother was smiling, her lips pursed tightly together. She seemed to have said all that she intended and Sheila found that she couldn't answer. What could she say? Instead, she gestured to the kitchen. "Isn't Mark eating, too?"

"Of course not," the mother said. "He eats like a bird all day—little bites and crumbs is all." She stuck her hand out and waved back at the kitchen as if to explain.

Mark came into the room with a bottle of wine stuck between his legs, his eyes on Sheila. Now that he wasn't wearing his mirrored sunglasses, Sheila noticed that his eyes were a deep, soft brown. When he wheeled his chair close enough to her, he grabbed the neck of the wine bottle and held it out in front of him as if he were a child who had just won a stuffed animal for her at the fair. "Here it is," he said. "Now everyone can eat."

He poured a glass for Sheila and then moved his chair back into a corner and watched the table. The mother scraped her teeth against her fork as she took small bites.

"Everything's wonderful," Sheila said. She turned and raised her glass to Mark.

"Oh, *it is not*. The catfish is cold and this cornbread is dry. Bigger pieces, I said." The mother reached up to her mouth and pulled something out with her fingers. She held the thin white bone, barely visible, up in front of her for Sheila to see. "Look," she said. She laid it on the edge of her plate and sighed.

Mark stayed in the corner and watched while Sheila ate. She could feel his eyes on her and so she ate more than she should have. When the mother complained, or coughed, Sheila remained quiet. The coughs would come from deep in the mother's chest, rough pauses that would leave her bent over the table. Mark, too, stayed quiet.

Sheila chewed her food slowly and tried to remember her etiquette. How quickly after dinner could she leave and still be polite? Would she be expected to ask them to dinner? She thought about her mother's dinner parties, with the blue linen napkins her mother taught her to fold in the shape of a bird. There were always after dinner drinks, then coffee, then more wine.

When Mark shouted at the mother, Sheila was just about to push her plate away and declare that she had eaten all that she could and that she wished she had room for more. She hadn't been paying attention, but she knew that the mother had just finished speaking. She could tell because the mother still had her mouth open and Mark had his eyes on her. Sheila felt her skin come alive, her own anger prickling up beneath the surface of the skin on her arms, underneath her velvet blouse.

"Does she know what you did?" The mother asked Mark.

The mother stood to mess with the lever on her oxygen tank and Sheila could see the line of her underwear when she bent over. Sheila stood up, too, and the napkin that had been on her lap fell to the floor. She looked at the small white heap and thought her mother would be proud. Not one stain, still as white as it had been when she unfolded it.

"It's getting late," Sheila said. Mother and son seemed to be at the start of a fight they had often.

"Please don't," Mark said.

"She knows about the about the girl and she still came?"

The mother turned and started to wheel her tank out of the room, then stopped and turned back to Sheila, her eyes hard. "You need to think before you just go to someone's house for dinner," she told Sheila. "You should think about what that *means* to a boy."

The tingling fingers, the heat on the chest. Sheila took hold of the fork next to her plate and squeezed the prongs into the fleshy palm of her hand. "He is not a *child*," Sheila said.

"See?" Mark said. He was looking at his mother now and his eyes didn't move away from hers. In his anger, Sheila could finally imagine Mark as he might have looked onstage with his band, his guitar slung across the front of his body.

"See how you always fuck things up?" he said.

The mother's face went pale and she picked at the edge of the rubber tubing from the oxygen tank, which dangled from one hand. "What a mouth you have," she said. "You watch yourself."

"I won't," Mark said. "You go to Hell." He stared straight at his mother and then his face pulled up and Sheila recognized the grimace; he was smiling. The mother turned away from her son and then looked surprised to see that Sheila was still there, watching them.

"Eighteen years old. I told his father not to buy him that car, too. But who listens to me?"

"It was an accident." Mark said, his voice quiet now.

The mother turned and walked out then, carefully, and the wheels squeaked until they hit the carpet in the living room and Sheila watched the tracks the tank made until the mother turned a corner and disappeared. Sheila felt relief, then, and when she heard a door slam she took a step away from the table and stared at the front door.

At her house she took off her clothes and lay down on her mattress, looking up and out the window at the sky. She hadn't yet gotten used to seeing the night sky so clearly, the stars spread out above her like a blanket, thousands of nail holes through thick, dark skin. She closed her eyes to try to sleep and she saw their imprint, still fresh. The stars disappeared behind her lids and then she saw the neighbor's hands, the balled fists and white knuckles.

Two weeks ago, on her way to Texas, she had picked up a man on the side of the highway somewhere in Arkansas. She had pulled over without thinking, before she could stop herself. The guy was a college kid, on his way back to school from the Christmas break. He carried a backpack and a duffel bag and called her *ma'am*. His hair was short and neat and he seemed overly clean. His sweater was a nice shade of blue.

When she asked him to stay with her in the motel, he seemed confused. *You're sweet*, he said. They were near Texarkana in the parking lot of a motel with warped siding that had started to fade from brown to plum in the baking sun. He followed her to the room and carried her suitcase. Then he stood by her door and thanked her for the ride. She watched him step carefully across the parking lot, between the puddles that had formed earlier in the day when a sudden storm blew through, before they had gotten there. She resisted the urge to chase him across the parking lot, right through the discarded fast food bags and used condoms and beer cans and make him come back to her room. Would she drag him? Beg him? Twist his arm behind his back? Or would she simply pull off her T-shirt, right there under the flickering fluorescent lights, and say please. Sheila liked to think she would have asked politely, but some part of her—the part that knew what she was capable of—forced her to turn back to her room, alone.

Sheila knew the truth about herself. She finally let herself realize what part of her—the honest part—had known all along, really: that she had meant to seriously hurt that girl. That she had wanted to hurt almost every child in that classroom.

She thought about the look on the mother's face when Mark had said the word accident, as if it were the one word that they'd agreed never to say out loud because they both knew it was a lie.

When Sheila woke up she was confused. She was cold and her back felt sore from the too-soft mattress. She sat up carefully. She could still smell the grease from Mark's house in her hair and on her skin.

Outside, in her driveway, she heard Mark's van. The tires slid fast on the gravel. She heard the engine turn off, then, a few minutes later, the door slam hard. She closed her eyes and waited to hear the hum of the wheelchair coming up the front sidewalk, and she imagined Mark in his chair, eyes on her front porch, waiting for her to come to him. There was the sound of a dog scratching at her front door, trying to claw his way in, and Sheila knew he would wait all night if he had to, maybe all month, all year, if that's what it took for her to come to him.

Bigger Than Love

It's two in the morning and I'm crouched behind the row of flat-topped, squat bushes that line the front porch of our house, watching my thirteen-year-old daughter walk our street naked.

Meg is running away from home, or at least trying to, but so far she hasn't made a turn off our block. Instead, she's spent the last twenty minutes walking to the corner, where the bulky blue mailbox sits, before pausing briefly and turning back. I hunch down on the wet concrete at the edge of our porch, the dampness soaking through the saggy bottom ridge of my nightgown, suddenly struck by the fear that Meg will get pneumonia from this middle-of-the-night parade of rebellion, or at least arrested if one of the neighbors happens to wake up. And what can I do about it? If I try to pull her back inside the house, she'll yell and kick and raise hell. And part of me knows that this attention is what this show in the street is really all about.

But if I'm honest with myself, I am sort of proud of the way she marches up and down our street, completely nude and not once bringing her arms up to cover her chest. If Meg wasn't my daughter, if she wasn't thirteen years old and naked and walking up and down our street in the middle of the night, I would be impressed with her posture, with the amazing way she holds her shoulders back. She's confident. Her body has transformed into something incredible, all legs and narrow waist.

When Meg starts to walk again, I crawl the few feet back to the front door and go in quietly. Then I sit in the living room, hand on the phone. Michael is still at the bar closing up. If I call him there and ask him to come home early, I know he'll put off the deposit—just drop the money bags into the safe in his office and wait until morning—and then he'll drive home fast, but not *too* fast, coax Meg from the street corner, wrap her in one of the blankets he keeps stashed in his trunk for emergencies, and then lead her to her room. Later, he'll ask if the neighbors saw. Because that's what we both worry about when you get down to it—embarrassing ourselves in front of the neighbors. We'll talk about the neighbors instead of what we should be talking about, which is the fact that sometimes I hate my daughter. That sometimes, in the middle of the night, after Meg and I have fought and I've had a lot of red wine—too much red wine—I tell Michael I want Meg gone in the morning. Not because she's run away, but because she never existed in the first place.

Poof, wisp of air, gone.

Earlier tonight, at dinner, Meg demanded a higher allowance so that she could buy *chronic*. (Then, when I pretended not to know what she meant, she said *ganja*. She rolled her eyes when I asked if she meant marijuana. "Pot," she whispered across the table at me. "Doobie. Smoke. Magic." She mouthed the words like a chant.) Then I looked at her and said, "Whose child are you?"

"Yours and some asshole's," she said. Then she threw her fork and I stared at her. It hit the wall behind me and then fell to the floor, clattering against the wooden planks. Meg never says anything hurtful about her father. I knew, though, that he called her last month to say that he'd gotten married again. He didn't tell me this news himself and neither did Meg. My mother called me the day after the wedding and told me about the girl he married. Eighteen years old and just graduated from high school, a student of his Georgia History class during her sophomore year. And when Meg asked if an eighteen-year-old was maybe a little too young, I kept my mouth shut.

I have never said one thing to Meg against her father, even during the divorce. I wanted out quick and clean and took only Meg with me and enough money to move to another state. Secretly, I've hoped that this new marriage will make Meg realize what I've been keeping from her all this time: that her father isn't the charming man she still thinks he is, the one who lets her tag along when he goes on summer vacation drives to Destin Beach and still calls her by cute, babyish nicknames. That, instead, he's the kind of guy that sends his daughter's calls to voicemail and marries an eighteen-year-old girl a few months after she graduates from high school.

And then Meg threw her fork and it hit the wall and fell to the floor by my feet. I picked it up. I felt the anger move into my chest and build up a wall, and wanted to know, felt that I deserved to know, exactly what he'd said to her.

I wanted to ask her, too, where she got her hands on drugs. I imagined Meg packed into a dirty bathroom stall at the roller skating rink, exchanging wadded bills for baggies of grass. Michael and I bought ours from a retired economics professor who grew his plants in an attic grow room, but when I thought of Meg, a seedy montage went through my head––complete with handshake drug exchanges, etc., etc. Brief snapshots from my own early teen years resurfacing, I knew, but still—and then Meg was up from the table and in her room pulling clothes out of her dresser drawers.

"I'm running away," she said. I stood and leaned against the doorframe of her bedroom and watched brightly colored bras get thrown into a giant duffle bag.

I watched her for a minute, wondering what to say. I tried to imagine what Michael would tell Meg if he were here but came up blank. "Those are all my clothes," I said, finally. "Everything you own, I've bought. So if you're going, you'll have to go naked."

Meg slid the bag under her bed. "Fine," she said. "I'll wait until it's darker outside, then."

I can't think of anyone to call except Michael and so I put down the phone and part the curtains, relieved to see that Meg has made her way back to our front yard now. She's standing underneath the Magnolia tree, where the neighbor's dog takes his morning break, her hands covering her face, and I want to go to her, hold her. She drops to her knees, wraps her arms around them, and starts to rock, and I'm about to get up from the couch, but then I see headlights coming around the corner and know—even before the car comes into view—that it's Michael. I close my eyes and count to ten. The phone rests in my lap. First, there's the sound of the tires on the gravel in the driveway, then the headlights shine through the curtains. The car door slams, there's Michael's feet on the gravel, his key in the lock on the front door. Finally, Michael turns on the light and I open my eyes.

"Your daughter is naked in the front yard," he says.

I cover my face with my hands and groan, roll my eyes in mock surprise. "Are you sure that's not someone else's angry teenager?"

He pauses, sighs. His feet shuffle a bit against the doormat. "I'll get her," he says. He sounds resigned, as if he's tasked with retrieving a naked Meg from the street every night. "Why don't you make her something hot to drink."

I get up from the couch and watch Michael go out to get Meg, let him help her off the ground, wrap his jacket over her shoulders, bring her into the house, into the kitchen.

"Let me talk to her," he says. I stand at the counter and pour microwaved water into a mug of powdered chocolate. Lumps float to the top and I poke them down with my finger. Meg sits in a chair at the table and stares at the floor, hugs Michael's jacket tight across her chest. I put a spoon in the mug and Michael takes it from me. On the front of his pearl snap shirt, there's a red stain from dipping his hand in the maraschino cherry jar at the bar. "Go to sleep," he says. "I'll be there in a minute." His voice is quiet, soothing, and I do what he tells me to. I go into our bedroom and close the door. In the kitchen, the chairs scrape against the floor and Meg's spoon clatters against the inside of her mug.

"I'm sorry," I say when Michael finally comes into the bedroom. He pulls open the snaps on his shirt, picks at the cherry stain. "I didn't know what to do. She asked me for drug money."

Michael doesn't seem surprised. "I think it's something else."

"Something with Nick?" Michael has always taken a hands-off approach with Meg's father, but this time, with the new marriage, feels different.

Michael shrugs, takes off his shirt, his pants. His legs still look a bit sunburned from the hike we took two weeks ago but the skin on his shoulders has peeled and healed, leaving a fresh patch of smooth pink skin. The elastic band on his boxer shorts is stretched loose and they sag a little on his hips, a reminder that I'd promised weeks ago to pick up a new package for him. He walks to the dresser on the other side of the room, opens the top right drawer where he keeps his socks and underwear, and brings back a joint. Almost immediately, my anger begins to float away from me, up towards the popcorned ceiling. We smoke the joint together in the bathroom like teenagers, the illegality of it making us happy again. Sometimes I wonder if Meg can smell it, if the tang of the smoke goes through the vents like the sounds we make when we're in bed, before Michael reaches up and covers my mouth with his hand. We huddle together by the bathroom window and watch the smoke float out through the screen of the window over the toilet.

After the joint's gone, Michael falls asleep quickly and I'm left staring up at the ceiling above our bed, imagining shapes in the reflections from the streetlamp outside. I look up at the dark shapes on the rough ceiling and give them structure. Snake, over there in the corner. Station Wagon. Submarine.

In the morning, Meg sits at the kitchen table, eating cereal and flipping through a magazine with a bunch of floppy-haired pop stars on the cover. She's dressed, I'm happy to see, in jeans and a sweatshirt. The sweatshirt is an old one of mine from college, with blue paint smears on both sleeves, at the elbows. Her hair is held up in a tight knot at the top of her head. With her lanky arms and blonde hair she looks nothing like me, but I have started to see a little of myself in Meg's movements, which are slow and awkward, and when she smiles she has the same dimple in her right cheek. The rest of her belongs to her father.

I look at the clock over the stove. "You're late for school."

Meg shrugs and pushes away her cereal bowl. "I've got a headache."

I go to the cabinet over the sink and push aside an army of bottles to get to the ibuprofen and I see the bottle of Paxil with its black box warning and Meg's name on the label. She stopped taking it last month, complaining of stomach cramps. "Why don't we take the day off?" Then, when Meg doesn't look up, I add, "We can take the bus over to Westside. Go to the mall."

Meg closes her magazine and gives me one of her looks.

"You mean let me skip school?"

"We can get lunch at that Chinese place, the one with the great egg rolls. Just let me get dressed." My voice becomes high, excited. Skipping school is something my own mother would have never allowed. I went to school no matter what; I would have to be hemorrhaging blood before she'd let me stay home. I know now, though, how hard it was for my mother to give up her time alone, during the day, the only time when the house was silent and clean. I imagine Meg and I laughing our way through the mall, maybe the bookstore. A montage of cheesy mother-daughter scenes spools its way through my head.

"No thanks." Meg gets up from the table and puts her cereal bowl in the sink. She ignores the bottle of ibuprofen I've been holding out to her all this time, like an idiot.

"It'll be fun," I say. "We can buy you a new swimsuit to take to your dad's."

Meg looks down at the bottle of ibuprofen, then at my over-bitten fingernails. "Are you joking?"

"Why would I be joking?"

"I just want to stay here."

I follow Meg into the living room. "You go to the mall or you go to school." The edge in my voice surprises me. When did this way of talking to her start? With her father's phone call? When she was caught smoking in the locker room before soccer practice? Meg clenches her jaw and stares straight at me but I don't look away.

"Fine." Meg walks down the hall and to her room. She slams her door and the frames on the wall next to me rattle, threaten to fall.

Meg says nothing to me on the bus. She sits across from me and pretends not to know who I am. When I try to say something, she looks around and wonders, with everyone else, who I'm talking to.

"Fine," I finally say, "be that way."

The woman next to me shifts her purse from one shoulder to the other. Her face looks tired and the skin under her eyes looks bruised. She looks like a wisened mother; the shoes she wears give her away—they're square, brown, built for comfort. I wear almost the same pair except mine are black. I avoided buying a pair for the longest time because, honestly, they're ugly as hell. And expensive. But God are they comfortable, with some sort of tilted footbed that supports the spine and makes you stand super straight, like a beauty queen. I wonder if this woman has a daughter and if she recognizes this situation. I get uneasy when I see a mother fight with her daughter at the grocery store, or in line at the post office. The arguments are too familiar. The daughters want to wear make-up, or they want their ears pierced. The mothers always look exhausted, worn thin. Their resistance has become a protective armor they wear like a second skin, and why not? They gave up on wearing fashionable clothing years ago, back when grunge was still cool. Now we wear shoes that make us look like we've got flippers.

We get off at the stop in front of Sears and Meg makes me walk around to the main entrance of the mall because she refuses to go in through that store. "It smells," she says, "like rotting cheese." Meg's tastes are expensive. She wears a pair of suede tennis shoes that cost more than last month's electric bill. Michael bought them for her. He has no resistance and gets her most of the things she asks for. I'm the one who's always saying no. Money isn't that much of a problem for us—not now that the bar is pulling a nice profit—but in the years before Michael came along it was something I worried about constantly and still do sometimes. Meg's father didn't have any money when we first got divorced and the support checks came from him in irregular spurts, always less than what they should've been. Now, even though he's got plenty of money, they still come whenever he feels like sending something. Then he gets on the phone and acts as if he deserves an award of some kind.

Michael always says we can afford to splurge every once in a while, but it's hard for me to spend money that isn't my own—hard for me to spend Michael's money on Meg. For Meg's eighty-dollar jeans, her sixty-dollar haircuts. But Michael thinks of Meg as his daughter, too, after all this time, even if we never get married. After our third date, he carried Meg in his arms from the backseat of his car to her bedroom after driving us home from a movie. She was the first child he ever held in his arms. He loved her like she was his own, he told me a year later, after we moved in with him. It hurts me to watch Meg take advantage of him. Meg knows he'll give her whatever she wants and I feel a pang of anger when I watch Meg work her way around me to get what she wants from Michael. Even when we were saving for the house, he found ways to cut corners to afford Meg's swim lessons, a new stereo for her room. Things her father wouldn't send money for.

Meg walks in front of me, shaking her hips. She walks like a woman. Her jeans are baggy and fall too low. When she reaches her arm up to fix her hair, the sweatshirt she's wearing comes up and I see the thin pink band of a pair of thong underwear.

I follow my daughter into a store with music so loud that I have to strain to hear the salesgirl who follows us around the racks. Meg pulls shirts off hangers and the salesgirl takes the pile into one of the dressing rooms. Meg doesn't come out when I call in to her. "Hey, come on, let me see," I beg, but she remains silent, the discarded clothes becoming a pool at her feet under the dark curtain that separates us. When she's finished, she pulls the curtain back and is dressed again in her jeans and my sweatshirt.

"Anything you like?" I ask.

"They all made me look huge." Meg's eyes are on my body, on the ring of fat that circles my waist and pushes against my blouse, threatening the buttons. I realize that Meg hasn't mentioned summer in Florida with Nick, the new clothes she should get to take with her, and I know suddenly that he has canceled her stay with him.

Meg leaves the shirts in a pile on the floor for someone else to pick up, just like she does at home.

I stop at the entrance to a lingerie store and call out for Meg to stop. She turns and comes back to me, then looks through the glass at the lacy negligee draped loosely on the mannequin in the window.

"How about that?" I ask.

"For who?"

"Me."

Meg looks again at the black satin straps, the lacy cups. She puts her hands on her hips. "You'd never wear that," she says.

I pull Meg into the store and buy the negligee straight off the rack, without trying it on. The flimsy satin feels light in the bag the saleslady hands me, like nothing at all, and I resist the urge I have to check to make sure that it's even in there. But Meg takes the bag from me and opens it on the way out of the store. She looks inside and separates the tissue paper the negligee is wrapped in. "It's pretty," she says, "but not your style." She hands the bag back to me and walks away, back out in front. I watch her through the group of mall walkers that power into the space between us. From a distance, my daughter looks like a stranger to me, like she belongs to someone else. She could be anyone's teenager, playing hooky from school and wandering around the mall, looking for trouble, and I try to imagine what kind of person Meg looks like to these strangers. I was never a serious troublemaker, but once I was picked up for shoplifting right before I turned sixteen. I slipped a bangle bracelet onto my arm when my friends went to the register to pay for their earrings and I can still remember the hand on my shoulder stopping me when I followed my friends out of the store. When I told Meg of my one-time arrest, my one moment of teenage rebellion, she didn't believe me. "You? Arrested?" she said. She crossed her arms and shook her head to let me know that she wouldn't be tricked. "Dad, maybe, but not you," she told me.

At lunch, Meg orders a root beer and Mandarin chicken. She's been walking away from me all day, leaving me behind corners, in restrooms. I've trailed behind her like one of the salesgirls. Now Meg is quiet and sips through a straw that's ringed with the red lipstick she sampled at the Clinique counter in Dillards. I refused to buy her the red, but, to keep peace, bought her a sixteen-dollar tube of frosted pink lip gloss. The paper bag sits on the table, next to her elbow.

"Can we talk?" I feel stupid asking this, like a television talk show host.

"About what?" Meg's voice is low, suspicious. She finally understands the point of this whole trip to the mall and this realization spreads across her face like a shadow. She grips her glass and prepares herself. There was a time, only a few years ago, when I couldn't stop Meg from talking to me. She would follow me around the house, tugging at my clothes and asking questions. She wanted to know everything. It would take me two hours to vacuum the living room because I'd have to keep turning off the vacuum to hear Meg's questions.

"I just want you to say whatever you feel like saying. About what's bothering you. I want you to talk to me."

Meg frowns and holds her lips shut tight. When she finally speaks, she looks away from me, out into the restaurant. "I don't feel like saying anything. There's nothing to talk about."

I hoped Meg would come out with a long confession of how her father had canceled their summer trip on the phone yesterday—how his new wife didn't want a step-child so close to her own age, maybe? But how would he have told her this, exactly? I want Meg to cause a scene, to cry, scream. I want Meg's pain to wash over me like some horrific emotional tsunami and this time I'll hold her, stroke her hair like I used to when she was a child and woke up from a nightmare.

Instead of talking about her father, though, Meg begins describing a pair of jeans a friend of hers from school just bought. Pre-dirtied, apparently, with factory-made rips at the knees, and Meg is the only one of her group who doesn't yet own a pair. She fiddles with the edge of the paper sack the lipgloss is in and when she tells me what the jeans cost I almost choke on my water.

"But what else?" I ask. "What about how you're feeling?"

Meg tears at the edge of the bag and shrugs her shoulders.

"I'm fine," she says, finally.

"You are?"

"*Yes*," she says. "Can we drop this now?"

I feel the wall but push it down, down. "I don't know what else to do, Meg. Why won't you talk to me?" I feel as if I'm about to choke.

"Buy me the jeans, then," Meg says, her voice flat. I realize she isn't making a joke and I have to press my lips tight to keep myself from yelling in the restaurant.

"You're selfish," I finally say.

"You are," Meg says back. Neither of us look across the table.

Then our food comes. Big steamy plates of fried wontons and battered chicken slathered in dark orange sauce. We eat quietly, our eyes lowered.

Michael comes home early. I can tell he's not sure what he'll find when he walks through the door by the way he looks around me, over my shoulder and down the hall. He was expecting a destroyed house, the aftermath of something big.

"Where's Meg?" he asks.

"In her room, on the phone." I laugh a little, a brittle sound that floats up in the air between us. "Talking to her drug connection."

Michael raises an eyebrow. "Anyone we know?" He pats my ass and goes around me, to the kitchen.

Meg's on the phone with her father but I don't tell this to Michael because he'll get angry and pick up the phone and ask if the jerk realized that he missed Meg's birthday, which was two weeks ago. Michael went out at the last minute and bought a new iPod and pair of bright pink headphones at Best Buy and told Meg that her father had sent them. Meg wasn't fooled, though. I saw the flicker of realization pass when she recognized Michael's handwriting on the card.

"What's for dinner?" Michael pokes around the refrigerator and I remember that I was supposed to get groceries, that there's a typed-out list Michael left for me on the dresser in the bedroom.

"Let's order a pizza," Michael says, letting me off the hook. "That sounds great, right? Pepperoni?" He shuffles through the pantry and retrieves the vodka from behind the row of canned vegetables, all those brightly labeled cans we never touch. I can't remember the last time I cooked something healthy in the oven, something not battered and fried or warmed up in the microwave, but I'm the only one who seems to suffer from the extra calories.

Michael pours us both incredibly large screwdrivers and we wait by the phone for Meg to blast the music on her stereo. This is how she communicates with us, how she lets us know that it's finally safe to pick up the phone.

The look that blossoms on Michael's face when I come out of the bathroom wearing the negligee is one I've never seen before—a half-smile frozen, eyes quickly averted, a look of pity. A few minutes earlier, when I slipped the silky fabric over my head in the bathroom, I realized it was the type of thing Meg's father always wanted me to wear for him. He'd buy me little g-strings, a feathery black nighty with matching garters for our anniversary one year. Things with tiny buckles and straps that made my face go red when I opened them up and held them in front of me. Even after I was pregnant, he'd bring this stuff home to me, wrapped in flowery paper, even though by then he avoided looking at my body—my thighs spread thick with blue veins, my ankles then as big around as my calves. I'd bring his hand to my stomach instead, to feel Meg move, and he'd pull away from me.

I looked at myself in the mirror and adjusted the straps on my shoulders. I felt big in the fabric; I'd gotten a size too small. Still, I felt sexy, like someone capable of feeling sexy. I thought about what Meg had said after I bought it, that it wasn't my style. That's what the look on Michael's face says when I step out of the bathroom and stand in front of him, at the foot of the bed, and I'm angry that Meg was right, that my daughter knows me better than I know myself.

"Where'd that come from?" Michael looks at me over the book he holds against his chest.

"Do you like it?" I stare down at myself, at the black lace webbed over my breasts. My nipples are visible through the sheer fabric and I feel suddenly exposed, embarrassed.

"It's different."

One of the straps falls off my shoulder and I let it rest against my arm. I start to take off the negligee, to change into my usual nightgown.

"No," Michael says, "leave it on. I like it, it looks nice." He puts his book on the nightstand and comes to me. He kisses my chest, then presses his lips into the soft dip at the base of my throat.

"I feel ridiculous," I say.

He puts his hand between my legs.

"I need this," I say.

Michael pulls me down on top of him, on the floor. The lacy fabric scratches my chest when he rubs against me but I leave the negligee on. "Should we smoke something first?" I ask.

Michael touches the fabric carefully, like bruised skin, and when he does this the wall inside finally breaks and I start to sob. I tell him about the Chinese restaurant and the expensive lipgloss, the jeans, the way Meg wouldn't look at me.

"Hey," Michael says. "Hey now."

"I can't do this anymore," I say. "I think maybe I'm done." I pull at the lacy ridge that cuts across the top of my chest.

He sits up and leans back against the side of the bed, takes hold of my hand. "You're right," he says. "Let's ship her off to the guy that just married the head cheerleader."

"I'm her hostage. If I give her a hundred bucks she'll set me free," I say.

"Not enough," he says. "A thousand."

"Five thousand."

"He's an asshole," Michael says. "She's a child."

"My child? My child asked for rocky road on the way home from swim practice. She held my hand when we rode the bus. I don't know who this is."

Michael stands up, makes his way to the bathroom. "Just love her," he tells me. "That's all we can do, right?"

But after he says that I realize that maybe loving her isn't enough. Not at all enough. That maybe what Meg needs is something bigger than love, something that gets captured in the photographs of the families in the J. Crew and Pottery Barn catalogues she obsessively flips through when they come in the mail, where an expensive and glossy illumination shimmers around the mother and father as they pose on a velvet sectional sofa, a toddler adorably positioned on the shag carpet near their feet.

Meg's gone by the time I get up in the morning and I walk around the house in the negligee, touching objects: the lamp on the end table by the sofa, the glass penguin figurine on the mantel over the fireplace. I can't remember buying any of the things on the shelves of this house—where did it all come from? I've been thinking about going back to work, or maybe back to school, now that Meg is older and isn't at home as much. Maybe I'll learn to cook. Maybe Michael can use me at the bar, during busy lunches.

I pick up a glass penguin and turn it over in my hands, feeling the weight of it. The penguin was a present to Meg from her father. For Christmas one year, when she was a child. I remember the look of confusion on Meg's face when she opened it. She held the thing in her hand by its head, dangling it in front of us both. She couldn't understand why he had gotten it for her. Meg and I were already moved to another state, away from him by then, and she was certain that I hadn't mailed her father her wish list in time—that the penguin she held in her hand was my fault. I lied and said I must have forgotten the list, which had included roller skates, a Barbie Dreamhouse, a new pair of ice skates. I had to promise to buy her a new dress before she would forgive me. Meg has come to accept objects as terms of forgiveness; the angrier she gets the more she expects you to spend. Her room is filled with apologies.

It's almost nine when the phone rings and the sound startles me. I drop the glass penguin and it rolls away from me, into a corner. The voice on the other end is deep and formal. Apparently, Meg's shorts are too short for school policy and I have to bring my daughter something else to wear.

"What happens if I don't?" I ask. Not to be resistant, I'm just curious. What would they have done if I hadn't been home? What happens to the students whose mothers work during the day?

"She'll have to wear something from the lost and found. A pair of sweatpants."

I think I hear Meg in the background, complaining, and I remember Meg's plea for the torn-up jeans. I feel tempted to tell them to make her wear the sweatpants. It'll kill her to wear someone else's dirty throw-away. Meg deserves the embarrassment, maybe, but where was I when Meg left the house this morning? Asleep in bed, this ridiculous negligee pushed up over my stomach. I tell the secretary I'll be there in fifteen minutes, the time it takes me to walk to the school.

  I slip an old terrycloth bathrobe over the negligee and look around on the floor of Meg's bedroom for a pair of jeans. There are T-shirts, two electric-colored bras, a brush, some socks. I stand in the middle of the room, frustrated, tugging at the belt on my robe. I walk to the laundry room, my head pounding. I imagine Meg at school, shorts up her ass, the rim of her thong slipped up over her hips, bumping through a crowded hall.

  I dig through the hamper and finally find a pair of Meg's jeans under a stack of wet towels. I walk barefoot out the door, slamming it shut behind me, knowing that something is wrong, that something's missing—that I've forgotten my purse, my house keys. I stand on the front porch, feet cold, in my open bathrobe and negligee, Meg's jeans a wadded damp ball under my arm. The breeze slips up my legs, blows against my chest, and I feel my heart pounding, the blood moving through my chest, up my neck and I know that what I'm about to do is wrong and that I should go back inside but instead I start to walk.

  I walk the four blocks to Meg's school, ignoring the glances of the neighbors walking their little puffy lap dogs with their be-ribboned ears and painted toenails clacking along, women pushing their plump babies in strollers on the way to the park in the opposite direction. I let the top of the bathrobe fall open, not stopping to cover my chest when the robe separates. I let the neighbors stare, at the way my breasts show through the lace, at my stomach, the way it pushes at the cheap fabric stretched across my skin.

  Meg sits on the front steps of the school, waiting alone. She isn't standing and pouty and angry like I expected. Instead, she sits hunched over, ball-like, and she's crying, even before she has a chance to look up and see what I'm wearing. Then Meg stands and I see that her shorts aren't what I expected, either. They're long, almost to her knees, in fact. They're the shorts Michael used to play tennis in, a pair she sometimes lounges around in on the weekends. She must have picked them up off the clean pile of clothing that I left on top of the dryer. Meg's eyes are red and swollen and when she sees me come towards her she drops her arms.

"Mom," she says, "why aren't you dressed?" She looks over her shoulder to the front door of the school and I look, too. Two women stare back at us through the plate glass window of the front office. I don't know what to say. I hold out the jeans. Meg takes a step towards me, her arm outstretched, then stops. "Just leave," she says. She starts to cry again. I fold the jeans and put them on the step in front of her.

"What's wrong with what you're wearing?" I ask her. "I think it's cute."

Meg looks back again to the women who still stare at us, their faces blurred in the window by the reflection from a grouping of trees. "Shorts are supposed to go past our knees," she says. "Because there's workmen here repainting the halls."

"So what?"

"So nothing." Meg bends down and picks up the jeans and I step back, away from her.

Meg looks up and the sun makes the pink sparkles from her new lipgloss glisten. Her knees, just at the bottom edge of the grey gym shorts, are scabbed over from a fall off her bike a week earlier. Her lipgloss has spread over the edges of her lips and the effect is a bit clownish, and I have a sudden flash of an eight-year-old Meg, at the circus, her lips stained from a cherry popsicle.

Meg lets her arms drop and the jeans come unfolded and she uses them to cover the front of her legs when she sees me staring at them. "Stop looking at me," she says.

"You're just a kid," I say, though I know that's not really true. I turn back to the school and the secretaries, who are still at the window, shaking their heads, almost in unison, and I know what they're saying to each other. I've been judged by women like them before.

"She's just a kid," I say again, but now I walk up the stairs and to the window where the secretaries are standing. I point back to Meg, who stands frozen on the steps.

"Mom," Meg calls after me.

"She's a child," I say, louder now. The secretaries look at each other to avoid looking at me, at my open robe and white, fleshy body beneath it. When I am almost at the window they stop looking at each other and stare straight at me. "A thirteen-year-old child," I say to the one on the left, the one with the dark brown hair and black-rimmed glasses. The woman stares back at me and I can see my own reflection in the glass between us. What I see before the secretary walks away from the window is a mess of hair and bare shoulders, the white flash of the open bathrobe, and Meg behind me, walking up to pull me away.

The Other Dorothy

When Alex's car pulled into the driveway, the headlights illuminated Dorothy—arms over her head, hair a large halo of thick dark curls, white cast up one entire leg. She wore underwear, the thick kind of cotton briefs little boys wear—the kind she's always worn—and a matching tank top stretched too tightly over her chest. She hobbled without crutches down the concrete path in front of the garage, the leg with the cast propped out to the side for balance. Alex stopped the car and took the keys from the ignition, but left the headlights on so he could get a better look at Dot when she walked in front of his car. He felt like he was back in high school, watching Dot perform in one of the terrible musicals she liked to take the lead role in. Alex sat and waited until Dot finally put one arm up over her eyes. Her eyes were covered, but her smile was wide, and her teeth glowed like the cast and the underwear, the front teeth out and over her bottom lip. In the cast, with the messed-up hair and the underwear, she did not look like her usually organized self. She looked like some creature that had crawled from the woods behind the house, a wounded animal trapped and frozen. She stopped in front of his car and stretched her arms out, balancing her weight against the hood of his car.

"Alex," she yelled, "Cut the headlights and help me around back!" She slapped the palm of her hand against the hood, then pushed herself back and followed the path around the corner of the house.

Alex clicked off the headlights and sat in the dark, twisting the ring of keys in his lap. There were no other cars in the driveway or along the street, and he thought about driving away. To the left, the house was lit up, windows open and curtains free. They brushed in and out of the boxed frames, sheer fabric that caught on the branches of the small lilac bushes that lined the front of the house. The house was breathing and Alex thought about the screens he helped to install last summer and wondered why they had been taken down. He took the missing screens as a sign that he should've turned the car around and gone back to Austin. Then called Dot or maybe Rudy in the middle of the night and apologized.

He sat and waited for Dot to come back around the side of the house, or for Rudy to come out to meet him. It was already past eight, and Rudy was probably inside, getting dressed, or at the liquor store in town picking up last-minute cases of beer, plastic bottles of bitter vodka and rum to spike the ceremonial punch. But no, Dot would have made sure that was picked up days ago. She would have figured and averaged alcohol consumption for each guest and written out a detailed list for Rudy, complete with exact numbers and prices figured with tax. Dot with her appointment calendars, her obsessive organization, her neat to-do lists taped to the side of the refrigerator. When it came to details and planning the woman was exact.

Nobody had said anything about a cast.

They told Alex first about the divorce before he got the invitation in the mail, the invitation to the de-wedding, the de-marriage celebration party that would end the one marriage he was certain would last. The invitations were beautiful and a creamy white, like their wedding invitations ten years ago. He'd helped Dot pick those out. They'd gone to a bridal exposition at the Austin Civic Center, and they'd chosen the invitations from a large book set out on a table. The invitation saleswoman had confused Alex for the groom, and when she'd asked his name he told her, and she'd written it down next to Dot's on the order form. When Dot laughed and explained who he was—brother of the groom, the best man, best friend of a girl he had known since they were kids and lived on the same block—the saleswoman had blushed and apologized. She wore a T-shirt with *Beautiful papers for a lifetime!* printed in red on the front. That made no sense to him—he imagined boxes of old newspapers and magazines stuffed away in an attic—but for some reason he felt comforted. The woman erased his name and wrote Rudy's in the cramped box of the order form, then talked about options— ink colors, graphics, the weight and texture of paper. Each decision seemed important, a test the paper lady administered to Dot, as if choosing the wrong font or inscription could predict future failures in the marriage. Dot made her decisions quickly while Alex stood to the side, inexplicably nervous, unable to look at the large piles of sample invitations the paper lady spread before them on the table. Behind them, two women argued about colors—white, cream, ecru. In her excitement, Dot had held his hand.

He'd helped Rudy, too. Two months before the wedding, the two of them drove four hours to a diamond wholesale store off I-35 in Dallas and picked out a wedding present for Dot. The manager was a sleazeball, a greasy-haired old guy in a gray suit who tried to push Rudy into buying a gold nugget pendant studded with diamonds. Rudy had always been into flashy things—the bigger the better—and Alex knew the manager could see the sucker in Rudy. Alex was determined to let Rudy choose his own gift, so he stood off to the side and pretended to examine a display of engagement rings. Then he saw Rudy consider the necklace, actually take the thing into his hands and run his finger over the unusually bright yellow cluster, and Alex pulled him aside and told him to think about Dot. He told him to think about the small earrings she always wore and the tiny pearl necklace her grandmother had given her. The manager frowned at him, and Alex thought they should have gone someplace else, but Rudy ended up buying a delicate pinky ring with a heart and a small diamond. On the drive home, they laughed about the look Dot would have given Rudy if he would have bought her the nugget. Rudy laughed until he started to cry, almost driving them off the highway once when he threw his head back to cough.

When Rudy failed to come out to meet him, Alex got out of the car, finally, and stood and looked in at the half-empty champagne bottle nestled between the two front seats. Their divorce present, which he drank on the drive even though he knew that would mean he'd show up empty-handed. He had stopped drinking over an hour ago, but when he shut the door to the car and stepped away he felt his legs shake, like after a ride on the Spinnaker at the county fair.

Behind the house, the yard looked beautiful, like the expensive houses on the north side of town at Christmastime. There were white lights strung up around the trees and over the backside of the house, pink lights draped over the side fence. Farther back, the woods looked dark and inviting. The massive stretch of wildlife seemed peaceful and a little dangerous.

Dorothy, still in her underwear, stood over a pile of wood in the middle of the yard and, as soon as she saw Alex, called him over to build the bonfire. She lingered behind him, balanced on crutches, giving directions.

"Pile the wood up into a triangle," she said. "*Jesus Christ.* You can't just throw everything in there. It's going to smother."

"What'd you do to your leg, anyway?"

Dot laughed. "I'm too embarrassed to tell you." Her hands fluttered in front of her face. Was she smiling? He saw a flash of white teeth between her fingers.

Rudy came out of the house carrying a pink bathrobe over his shoulder. He walked up behind Dot and draped it across her shoulders then held out his arm so she could balance herself while she slipped her arms through the sleeves.

"Alex," he said, "I didn't hear you drive up."

Alex squatted down on the ground and criss-crossed twigs into a pyramid. "Where is everyone? I thought this thing was starting at eight."

"Nine, Alex. For you we made up a special invitation so you'd show up on time." Rudy came and stood over him, inspecting. "You should know better than to listen to Dot when it comes to building a fire." He bent down next to Alex and rearranged the logs on the bottom of the pyramid and the whole pile tumbled.

"Oh, Rudy. That was a work of art and you ruined it." Dot said this and stared at the pile of twigs with a frown on her face. Then she went away. She swung herself across the yard, past the long table of Jello molds, pigs in blankets, and hamburger patties. Her robe came undone and slipped off one shoulder.

"She's been a wreck all day," Rudy told him. "This party has her crazy."

"What's up with the cast?"

"She didn't tell you?" Rudy laughed and the sound came from deep in his throat, a mean chuckle. He pulled at the pieces of wood, piled them into one big stack, making a mess of the neat pile Alex had tried to please Dot with. He'd always had the need to please her. She'd always bossed him around and he'd let her. He liked it. In grade school, he had been the first on their block to get a crush on her, years before Rudy, and she'd used that power over him whenever she had the chance. Rudy still teased him about the time Alex came home with his face smeared with lipstick and rouge, Dot's attempt at creating a sister for herself.

Rudy tossed wood on top of the pile and the pieces fell down the sides until he said, "Fuck it, good enough," and stood up. Alex stood up with him and they both stared down. Alex thought of Boy Scout camping trips and Rudy's obsessive need for perfect fires. He couldn't believe Rudy was ready to light the mess he had made.

"Well?" Alex asked. He went back to thinking about Dot and the cast. He imagined Dot falling off the mechanical bull at the bar they owned, or falling off the ladder while cleaning the gutters.

"It'll light up well enough."

"I mean the cast, Rudy."

"Right," he shook his head and exhaled. "Skydiving."

Alex waited for the joke. Dot's fear of heights kept her away from roller coasters and tall buildings. She wouldn't stay in hotel rooms past the sixth floor. There was no way she would jump from a plane. That was what Alex said to Rudy. He said there was no way Dot would jump willingly from a plane.

"She did!" Rudy said. There was pride in his voice, and a gentleness with it. "Just a problem with the landing, nothing serious."

"But why?"

"My divorce present to her. Guy over at the airstrip in Temple takes you up for fifty bucks. It's a steal." Rudy took his lighter out and bent over the pit. He lit the pieces of wadded-up newspaper threaded in between the logs at the bottom of the pile. He lit every piece he could get to, then stepped back and admired the flames. "See? That's gonna work. That'll light up just fine."

Alex's head felt heavy and the smoke from the fire burned his eyes. The wind started to turn chilly and waves of cool air mixed in with the hot rush from the fire. "Did you jump too?"

"No," Rudy said. "Why would I?"

"Why not?"

"She gave me a different present."

"Divorce presents?"

"Yeah, we figured since wedding presents build a life together that divorce presents should take something away. So Dot jumped out of a plane."

"What did you do?" Alex could hear the sarcasm in his own voice, the slow pause between words.

Rudy slipped his hands into the front pockets of his jeans.

"Slept with another Dorothy."

Alex was about to say something, but then there was a crash from inside the house and Dot's cry. Rudy was across the backyard and into the house before Alex could move.

Two months earlier, they had called in the middle of the night, both of them talking to him at once, explaining. Dot was on the phone in the kitchen and Rudy was on the cordless. Alex could hear Rudy's voice and the rumble of a train that was going by across the road that went in front of their house. It was late.

"But why?" he asked them. He wanted a clear explanation, a solid timeline of events that would show him the breakdown of their marriage. In his pool of divorced friends, Rudy and Dot had been proof that two people could come together and make love work. But more than that Rudy and Dot were his family, what was left of it. The ones who took him in for holidays and vacations. All of the men in Alex's family had divorced their wives, abandoned their kids, and Rudy had become a comfort to Alex. He'd been the one man who hadn't given up.

"It's just something that's happened," Rudy said.

"We're different people." Dot's voice was louder than Rudy's, clearer. "You're there and you just can't see."

It struck Alex that this breakup was her idea. Dot acted on impulse and Rudy let her have what she wanted. This ability of Rudy's to compromise had been one of the reasons Alex felt relieved he hadn't tried for Dot back in high school. Alex had made a list of reasons back then stating why Rudy made a better fit with Dot. "So let me drive up this weekend and we'll talk about this. We'll work it out. Different people? That's a cliche, right? We're all different people."

"There's nothing to work out. This has been coming for a long time, Alex." Dorothy exhaled when she said this, her way of warning him to drop the questions. Her voice sounded tired.

"Why can't you try a separation?" Alex's voice cracked, and Dot cooed to him.

"Sweetie," she said, "Alex, baby. It's okay, we're okay with this."

He hated her then. He hated her smooth, clear voice.

"Nothing's going to change," Rudy said. Alex could hear the click of his lighter and then his exhalation. Dot wouldn't let him smoke in the house. He imagined Rudy outside on the porch, shivering in boxer shorts, and Dot inside the warm kitchen, eating chocolates and drinking brandy from one of the expensive crystal glasses Dot's mother had given them for their anniversary last year.

"I'm confused," he told them. "I need to think."

He avoided their calls for over a month while he tried to get used to separating Rudy and Dot. He thought he'd be able to support them finally, and take part in this divorce whole-heartedly. During his divorce, which was bitter and lasted longer than the marriage itself, Dot and Rudy had been there for support. They didn't know his wife that well, had only met her at the wedding and at a few dinners after that, but when it was all over they had told him what he wanted to hear. That the woman he had married was manipulative, not worthy of his love, a horrible creature he could live better without. He had married that woman he barely knew because he thought it could bring him what Dot and Rudy had. He didn't tell them that. He didn't tell them that he failed at his marriage but comforted himself with his role in theirs. After Alex had given up on his chances with Dot, there seemed to be an unspoken rule that Rudy would repay him by allowing Alex into their life together.

Seeing Dot in her underwear, standing in her own backyard, made Alex feel as if this were his divorce that was about to happen and Rudy wasn't doing anything to help.

Inside, Dorothy was on her back on the linoleum floor in the kitchen with Rudy on the floor with her, his knees next to her head. Dot's robe was open and spread out beneath her. Rudy stroked her hair and held her hand. "Dorothy," he said. "Dottie pie."

Dorothy looked at Alex and smiled, but then her face squeezed together like a fist: her eyes closed, lips came together, forehead wrinkled. She let out another cry that was unlike anything Alex had ever heard.

They had become animals, both of them. There was Dot and her wailing, which kept going and became louder, and then she brought her arms to her chest. Rudy pawed at her hair, smoothing it against the floor, away from her face.

"Help me get her up," Rudy said. He looked around the room, trying to decide where to move her. "To the table," he said finally.

"Maybe we should call an ambulance," Alex told him, as if Dot weren't in the room with them. "She might've hit her head and they say you're not supposed to move people with head trauma."

"I don't know," Rudy said to him, then he turned back to Dot. "How about it, Sweets? Your head hurt?"

Dot wailed and Alex went to the phone. When he picked up the receiver, she opened her eyes and turned to look at him. "Stop it! I'm fine. Just get me off this floor." She gritted her teeth and then turned again to Rudy. "It's freezing. I'm cold." Her eyes were red, and her face had gotten puffy. On the side of her stomach, Alex could see the scar from when she had her appendix out when she was a teenager and was a cheerleader for their high school. She had worn orange polyester then, and a skirt with black trim. The scar was ugly and white against her brown stomach. She was thinner than he had ever seen her, but he was not used to seeing her undressed. Maybe she had always been like this. Her ribs were thick fingers coming up.

It occurred to him that she was sick. He thought she was about to die and they hadn't yet decided on the right way to tell him. He thought cancer, AIDS, one of the terrible diseases he saw on television. He thought he was the last one to know.

"Are you dying?" he asked. "Is that what this is about?"

Rudy stopped helping Dot and they both stared at him. Rudy's mouth opened. "What are you talking about?" he asked. "What the hell kind of question is that?"

Alex pointed to Dot's stomach and the scar as if to explain. He didn't answer. Dot wrapped the bathrobe over herself and tied it. "Nothing's wrong with me," she said. Her voice was small and quiet in the room. Alex couldn't get the image out of his mind of Dot in a hospital bed, head wrapped in gauze, bruises over her body like spots on bad fruit.

Someone knocked on the front door and the three of them froze. In the moment of revelation Alex had forgotten about the divorce party, the groups of people.

"You get it, Alex." Rudy said. He pulled the edge of the bathrobe carefully over Dot's legs but Dot pushed his hand away.

"I want to get dressed." She wrapped her fingers tightly around Rudy's arm and pulled him close to her. "Help me get dressed?"

In Dot and Rudy's backyard, there were people Alex hadn't seen since the wedding. Annie Clayton had been a cheerleader with Dot, and now she was a large woman with yellow hair who stood next to the grill and ate a cheeseburger. Alex talked to her.

"I'm divorced, too," she said.

"Aren't we all?" He had a can of beer, and he let the coldness of the can numb his fingers. He stared over Annie's shoulder at the black density of trees behind her.

He swore that he saw something move behind one of the trees close to the edge of the backyard. An animal. A big dog, perhaps, or maybe a deer. He thought he saw brown fur.

"It doesn't surprise me, though." Annie finished her cheeseburger and wiped the palm of her hand across her stomach.

"What are you talking about?" The animal was gone. It retreated back into the darkness. He looked back at Annie's face, which had become fat and round and a little sad. Her red lipstick was smeared on one side and there was sweat along her hairline. Alex couldn't imagine how she had come to look like this. Had she actually gotten shorter, too? She wore a pink ruffled dress that looked like the curtains his ex-wife had put up in their bedroom. They'd fought about those curtains and he had lost. They stayed in the bedroom and he left.

"We stray from God. No one cares." She pouted, and he had to look away from her again. She had become one of the over-bearing adults he had grown up with in Waco—quick to ram religion down your throat while they acted superior. What had God given her? A divorce and polyester tent dresses to cover her stomach? Who was she to judge anyone? If he hadn't turned away then he would have punched her. Well, maybe not a punch, but he liked to think he might have hit her in the face—not too hard—across one of her swollen cheeks. Then she cracked up laughing and hit him in the arm. "God, Alex. Did you think I was serious?"

He went into the house to find Rudy. Even after he closed the door, he could still hear Annie's laugh over the crowd of people talking. It was a high-pitched squeal filled with desperation and the sound made him nervous. Maybe his fear wasn't from the sound but from Annie's pink dress, the shade of it, which made him think of a pig about to be slaughtered. The pig made him think of the filmstrips they used to show in Sunday school, the cartoon ones with all the animals gathered around the tiny wooden crib in the manger, and with a shock he realized that Annie had gone to the same church as he and Rudy, had even sat in the back with them and thrown spit balls at the white wall they used for a movie screen.

Dot sat at the kitchen table alone, drinking a beer. She had changed into a white dress that looked like a nightgown, and Alex thought for a second that she had changed her mind about the divorce, and the party, and instead was about to go to sleep. Then he saw the veil on the table next to the can of beer, and he realized that she was wearing the same dress she had worn for her wedding, the one her mother had made for her from the fabric Dot had picked from a catalogue. It looked thinner now somehow, less substantial than the dress he remembered.

On the table was the stack of papers, the divorce papers that had been sent over earlier in the day. Rudy had shown them to him while Dot was in the bedroom getting dressed. They were selling the house and splitting the money. They would continue to own the bar together but Dot would run it. Rudy wanted to travel. When he told Alex that, he pictured Rudy in the Australian outback, a safari cap perched on his head. Alex pictured Rudy building campfires in countries with strange languages.

"They've turned into people I don't recognize," Dot said. "A bunch of cows." She took a sip of her beer and picked at the edge of the label on the bottle. "Is there enough food out there? Do things look okay?"

Alex thought of the long table of half-eaten hotdogs and potato chips, the bowls of Jello with missing chunks, the small piles of dip punctuating the tablecloth. "Where's Rudy?"

Dot sighed and took a drink from her beer. Some of it spilled on the front of her dress but she didn't wipe it up. "He's getting into his suit. You should help him with his tie."

"Are you really going through with this?"

"It's out of my hands." She held her hands up in front of her so he could see. She was emphasizing her point. She'd learned to use her hands for emphasis in her public speaking course in high school. It was a quirk of hers that made Alex want to scream.

"No, it's not." His voice had that edge to it, the sarcastic anger that had made Dot smile at everything he'd said so far that night. "Of course it's not."

"Go help your brother," she said. "Make yourself useful."

Alex realized that Dot was talking to him as if he were a child, in that slow voice she used when she spoke through her half-smile.

Rudy was in the bathroom, sitting on the counter next to the sink. He had the window open and was smoking a cigarette. He looked at the people who were filling the backyard.

"I don't remember sending out this many invitations. Were there this many people at the wedding?" He wore a brown suit and his cowboy boots, which were old and worn, the bottoms caked with dried mud. In high school he was in the junior agriculture program and he'd wanted to be a rancher. He'd shown a heifer at the state fair in Dallas in 1997 and had won best of show. He was famous in Waco that summer, the king of the ag program, the sweetheart of cow lovers. Dot hated that.

Rudy kicked his heels against the cabinet doors and clumps of mud fell to the floor, onto the piece of white shag carpet that served as a bath mat.

"I don't remember."

"We should've had this thing at the bar, but Dottie didn't want to shut it down on a Saturday night. Too much money lost." Rudy finished his cigarette and threw it into the toilet. It sizzled then floated with three others. He fiddled with the handle of the toilet and a hollow metal clank and then a whine came from somewhere inside the top of the tank. Rudy frowned. "Why aren't you outside?" Then, "Where's Dot?" He looked worried, like she had suddenly disappeared and left him alone with a backyard full of people.

"In the kitchen. Getting drunk." Alex didn't know why he said this. Dot never got drunk. They owned a bar and she never had too much to drink. He'd seen her drink too much only once before, back in high school. After Rudy's heifer won and they drove the thing back to Waco together. Rudy pulled into the high school parking lot and Dot opened the truck door and vomited, then passed out. Rudy showed off his ribbon and let the girls poke at the neck of the heifer through the wooden slats of the trailer.

"I want you to stop this break up," Alex said.

"Want me to what?" Rudy looked confused.

Alex thought about the way Rudy's face got when he was angry, the way his lips pressed together and his cheeks bulged. He thought of Dot's fisted face.

"You don't love her?"

"Of course I do. What, you think I could stop?" Rudy, offended, held one hand up to his chest and backed away. Alex had hurt his feelings. "How could you even ask me that?"

"Okay, then, what's this about?"

"We told you."

"Tell me again."

"Jesus Christ. You got all night?" Rudy laughed a little, then shook his head.

"Sure, yes. I've got all night." Alex laughed, too, but then he dropped his head and looked to the ground.

"Listen, we're not keeping anything from you. There's no big secret here, Alex. I need to get away from this place. Dot wants kids and I don't. We're getting older and we've just grown apart." Rudy exhaled and stepped around him. Alex smelled the cigarette smoke and, underneath that, Rudy's aftershave. It was the same scent they had both worn in high school, the woodsy pine aftershave that left their skin burning after baseball practice when they'd leave the locker room and meet the girls in the parking lot after school to go to the mall. The sweet smell of a forest in decay.

Alex rolled his eyes but Rudy was already out of the bathroom, out of the bedroom even. Alex could hear the heels of his boots on the wooden floor of the hallway.

"Sweets!" he called, "Dottie!"

"In here," she yelled. "Come get me!"

In the kitchen, Dot and Rudy sat across from each other at the table. They looked away from the stack of papers between them. Dot stared at her veil and Rudy's eyes were on the clock above the refrigerator. Dot's cast was propped up on the other kitchen chair. The bottom of it looked filthy, and there was a wedge of rubber glued onto the bottom. To Alex, the rubber wedge looked like a blue eye staring straight through him.

The vision came to Alex in a flash. He saw Rudy pushing Dot down the stairs at the bar, or off a ladder. He saw Dot's arms bent and slapping at the air as she fell, like she was swimming. Rudy wasn't violent, his temper had always been even, but maybe Dot had provoked him. Maybe she told him she didn't love him anymore and he'd lost his senses for a few seconds and the accident had happened.

"I know what this is about," he said. He stood across the kitchen and looked from one to the other. They both looked up at him at the same time. "It's the broken leg, right?" He stared at Rudy. "You did it."

Rudy was up and across the kitchen before Alex could get away. Rudy pushed him back against the refrigerator, his forearm against Alex's throat. His other hand became a fist in Alex's stomach. Rudy didn't punch, but he pushed it hard into Alex's gut. Air escaped from Alex's mouth in a quick gasp.

Alex could smell Rudy's breath, the cigarette smoke, and whiskey under that. Rudy stared straight into Alex's eyes, and he could see the hate in them, and the pain. Alex tried to remember the last time they had fought and whether or not Rudy's eyes had narrowed then the way they were now. Alex couldn't remember, though. All he saw was a mosquito-bitten arm smacking against his chest when they were twelve years old and on a camping trip. He tried to think if they had ever fought as adults, and when he realized that they hadn't, he knew he was wrong about Rudy hurting Dot. Rudy leaned in closer and his lips were chapped and parted and there was a thin sliver of blood in the meaty inside of his lower lip. Alex tried to take a deep breath but the fist pushed harder and he stopped trying to struggle, helpless.

"Rudy!" It took Dot a long time to get to her feet. She came across the kitchen to them, her arms outstretched. There was desperation in her eyes; her mouth was open. She put a hand on Rudy's shoulder but he pushed his forearm harder against Alex's throat.

For a few seconds, Alex couldn't breathe.

"Take it back!" Rudy said, as if they were children calling each other crude names in the parking lot at school. Alex shook his head and leaned back against the refrigerator. "You take that back," Rudy said again. Rudy looked twelve-years-old again, and Alex started to laugh just as he had when they were children.

"Alex!" Dot looked over Rudy's shoulder at Alex, her eyes wide. "What's the matter with you?" Her voice shook. He opened his mouth to say something, but his voice was gone. A rattle came out instead, a low string of vowels that floated in the air. Dot squeezed Rudy's shoulder again and he released Alex. Rudy's face looked red, and swollen, and he shook his arms.

"Take it back," he said again. He looked away from Alex, as if it was something he had to do in order to stop himself from going for his throat again.

Alex opened his mouth, helpless. "I do," he said. "I'm sorry. I just..." He coughed and put his hand across his throat.

"What?" Rudy's eyes were on the floor. "What?"

"I don't understand," Alex said. Then, "She chose you."

Dot went to Rudy and wrapped her arms around him, buried her face in his chest. He held her and stroked her hair. Alex stood to the side and watched them together and realized they were strangers to him. They had become unpredictable to him and he had never imagined that would happen.

"Just go outside," Dot finally said, her voice muffled. "Make sure the keg's working and the food's okay."

Alex felt ridiculous. His stomach hurt and he realized he was going to be sick. He started to walk to the bathroom.

"Outside," Rudy said.

Alex held up his hands, Dot's gesture. "Okay," he said. "All right." He backed away from them and went out the back door. Dot followed him. They stood on the concrete landing, under the yellow bug zapper. She cornered Alex and, out of protection, he covered his face with his hands.

"What's the matter with you?" Dot's voice was a slow, mean whisper.

Alex dropped his hands and held them at his sides. In the yellow light Dot's face looked golden and beautiful again. "You made him sleep with another woman," he said finally. "And he made you jump out of a plane. Doesn't that seem a little unreasonable?"

"We're adults, Alex. Nobody *made* us do anything."

Rudy came to the door, pressed his face to the glass, and stared. Alex felt guilty. "I'm sorry," he said. Rudy knocked on the glass and Alex repeated himself, louder.

"Grow up," Dot said. "Think about somebody else's feelings for a change." She swung herself away from him and went back inside. The screen door slammed and he stared in through the door at the two of them, Rudy holding Dot and cupping the back of her head. Rudy stared over Dot's shoulder at Alex, his lips pressed tightly together.

Alex turned and looked over the backyard, and the party guests—the people he knew from his past—seemed to be laughing at once. There were people everywhere with their mouths open, their teeth glowing. He walked through the crowd and stood at the edge of the yard. His legs went weak and he let himself drop on the wet grass. The coolness of it soaked through his pants and rested against his hot skin.

His anger floated from him and he looked out at his forgotten high school friends. They were blameless, forgiving, a crowd of people who had come to expect failure in love. He saw them all. He sat there and listened to the animals behind him, moving around in the branches, and thought of his wife. He thought of the afternoon that she asked him to leave the house and how he had sworn later to Rudy that he could feel every word she had said settle on his skin like hard pellets of sleet. He'd left her without a word. He'd packed up two suitcases and she followed him around the bedroom, her fists clenched at her sides. *Aren't you going to say anything?* She'd asked. *Aren't you going to ask why?* He'd moved through the rooms of their house quietly, picking up socks and newspapers, random things, and carried them to the open suitcases on the bed. He had felt a sense of relief; an expectant calm had settled somewhere inside of him and kept him quiet. On his skin, though, he felt the prick of her words and the cut from her eyes.

Before he left the house, the two suitcases waiting on the front porch, he stood staring out the front door and his wife came up behind him and pushed him hard. He stumbled into the glass, the side of his face hitting against the cool flatness. When he turned to confront her she was already walking away, her fists unclenched and fingertips brushing easily against the folds of her skirt. The next time he saw her, she couldn't look at him without smiling. Her grin was pasted on but her eyes were brittle blue stones that had turned a shade darker and were full of hate. They were at her lawyer's office and Alex signed the papers without looking up at her. He let his own lawyer speak for him and he said nothing. He kept his eyes on the table, and then he left the office and went back to the apartment with no furniture. He could feel her hands on his back that night, and when he thought of her he imagined her eyes as cold stones that she plucked out and threw at him. They bounced off his chest and fell to the ground. His wife stood before him, eyeless, smiling. *We can't all be perfect*, she had said. *Not everyone's perfect.*

Alex stood up, finally, and looked back at Dot and Rudy's house. All of the lights were on inside and the house glowed. If he had been feeling optimistic, he could have made a nice metaphor of a house on fire with passion. He stood at the edge of the yard and looked over the crowd. Annie Clayton had found the minister. She moved her arms when she spoke and her eyebrows rose and descended when she smiled and frowned. The minister was fifty and balding; he had a piece of white toilet paper wrapped around his neck which served as a clerical collar. Annie stood close to him, her hand on his arm for balance. Through the padding, she was still the cheerleader; she knew how to smile and nod her head with enthusiasm. Alex could see the hope on her face and the anger in her eyes for every man who had ever dumped her.

It was past eleven already, and Rudy and Dot had yet to come out of the house. The minister stood next to the back door with Annie and when someone got too close to the back steps he held up his hand and shook his head. The toilet paper collar had given him the authority to boss the crowd around. When Alex tried to move to the back door to sneak inside the house, the minister looked away from Annie and started towards him. When Alex stopped, the minister stopped.

"I'm Rudy's brother," Alex said, finally.

"Doesn't matter who you are. We're about to start things," he said. "No one's supposed to go in there."

Alex stepped back and retreated into the group of guests. The backyard was filled with people he didn't quite recognize. The man pumping the keg looked like his baseball coach from high school, Coach Agsley. In the dark it was hard to say if it was him, though. This man looked fuller, softer. When he pumped the keg his cheeks puffed and Alex swore he heard him grunt. There were people everywhere. They bumped past him, their voices thick in his ears. The woman next to him tugged at the sleeve of his jacket. When he turned, she held a cigarette up and raised her eyebrows.

"I don't suppose you got a light?" She had the thickest drawl he'd heard since high school. Pure Waco flatness with a blend of vowels. The sound was rough music in his ears, the comfort of home. Her hair was dyed a bright yellow and straw-stick straight. She looked like an older version of every girl he had longed for ten years ago. Every girl except Dot.

He shook his head and she pouted.

"Dorothy!" The minister broke away from Annie and came to Alex, or looked like he was. "Dorothy, sweetheart." Alex looked behind him, expecting to see Dot's face looming over his shoulder, but there were only trees behind him, the dark edge of the woods. Dorothy was the woman next to him. She opened her arms and the minister wrapped his around her waist. The toilet paper tangled in the woman's hair and came undone when she pulled away. The strip floated between their two bodies then settled in the grass.

The other Dorothy.

She turned back to Alex and something in her eyes made him nervous. "Do I know you?" she asked.

"I don't think so." But he recognized her now, though when he first met her years ago, at the bar, her hair had been short and brown, the color of mud. Dot had introduced her to him as "the other Dorothy" and they had all laughed at that. This Dorothy was divorced, too, he remembered. With three kids or maybe even four. One of them had been in the stock room at the bar that night and he was introduced to Alex as "special." The kid had worn a scratched football helmet strapped to his head. Dot had sat in the backroom coloring with the boy and, when Rudy had asked Alex to run back and grab more napkins, he walked in on the two of them sitting cross-legged on the floor, crayons spread between them like a blanket. The boy had drooled and rolled his eyes at Alex, unable to focus. *He's special*, Dot had said. *A perfect special boy.* Dot had stared at the boy with love, as if he were the only person in the bar, and Alex thought about what Rudy had said about Dot wanting kids.

Dorothy narrowed her eyes and tilted her head. He imagined Rudy's hands in this Dorothy's yellow hair and her legs wrapped around his waist. He imagined the two of them in a room at the La Quinta off the highway, cigarettes smoldering in a cheap glass ashtray on the nightstand, both of them naked on the polyester bedspread. He imagined Dot arranging the room, picking Dorothy from the other waitresses, offering her a bonus of extra vacation time or maybe money.

He thought of Rudy in bed with this other Dorothy, and then he saw Dot falling from the sky, her leg bending sideways as she hit the ground.

He thought of this Dorothy with yellow hair and the look she must have had on her face when Dot asked her to sleep with Rudy. To please sleep with her husband, who had not slept with any other woman except Dot. Ever. This new Dorothy who would be the first in a series of women, the one to get the ball rolling. The first woman Alex had slept with after his own divorce was a big woman he picked up at a dance club in Austin. He had taken her back to his apartment and she had walked through the empty rooms, had stared at the bare walls. Later she felt like wet dough beneath him, soft and forgiving. She helped him to forget the sharp angles of his wife and he was grateful.

But this Dorothy looked thin and mean, a slightly larger version of Dot. The bones in her face were smooth and angled, sharp at the edges. Then she smiled and her face softened. The face went all wrong: her right eye drooped, a deep dimple puckered her cheek, and her nose flattened like someone was pushing down on it with the tip of his finger.

Dorothy's eyes widened and she focused on his face, took in his thinning hair, his long nose. "Alex," she said, smiling. "Remember? I met you at the bar a few years ago."

His eyes closed. The face of the special boy moved in front of him, all drool and pink cheeks. Alex opened his mouth to say something but the minister's voice came over him like a wave.

"Music!" the minister yelled. Alex opened his eyes and Dot and Rudy were coming down the steps from the back door of the house. Annie pushed the play button on a beat-up tape recorder and the wedding march played. The crowd groaned and laughed. A few people cheered. Rudy and Dot moved past him, both smiling. They didn't see him. They kept their eyes focused on the center of the yard, where the minister had cleared a small circle. Rudy had his arm around Dot's waist, and he guided her to the center, through the thick of arms that blocked their path.

Dorothy tugged at Alex's sleeve and when he turned to her he saw that she was crying. Her eyes were glassy and her cheeks were wet. The white lights from the side of the house blinked across her face, forming a pattern of stars on the smooth space above her eyes. She still held the cigarette, unlit, between her fingers.

"Do you have a car here?" she asked. "Can you take me home?" Her eyes roamed his face, took in the scar above his right eye, the dark shadow on his jawline, then settled on his own eyes. He thought he could see straight into her soul, which was open and raw and a little weepy. He looked for guilt and he saw that there, too. Her hand was still on his sleeve, and he felt the heat of her against his arm.

"Now?" Alex asked. He turned and saw Rudy and Dot, who now stood in the center of the yard. Dot's hands were over her eyes again and Rudy was looking down at the top of her head. Both of them were laughing but Alex saw, on Rudy's face, the same angry look that he had seen when he had pushed him against the refrigerator. In that look Alex saw the years in this house, in this suffocating town, and he heard Dot's low voice asking this other Dorothy to sleep with her husband. Her request a plea, voice filled with desperation. And maybe Dorothy saw the desperation and felt the need to help, to do what she could to take that away.

Or maybe not. Alex thought that maybe he was getting the story wrong again. Maybe what Dorothy thought was that she could break this marriage apart for good, cause a split that would leave her comforting Rudy and hating Dot for a very long time. Maybe this was what she was crying for, and when she looked at Dot and Rudy she didn't see the look of anger on Rudy's face. She saw Rudy's arm around Dot's waist, supporting the woman he loved, the woman he would always love, no matter how many women he slept with. No matter how many Dorothys came into his life.

Alex reached up to wipe under Dorothy's eye. She brushed his hand away and shrugged. "It's nothing," she said. "I always cry at divorces." She smiled and her face broke apart again, the sharp angles went flat and the meanness floated from it and settled above them.

He put his arm around her waist and the two of them stepped back into the dark woods. They slipped out of the yard without detection and disappeared into the blackness with the animals. The weeds were thick, waist-high, but there was a dirt path that went around to the front of the house and they followed it. Dorothy was hot against him and she rested her head on his shoulder. He put his hand in the middle of her back and guided her through the mess of branches.

"I'm not sure if I'll sleep with you," Dorothy said. "That's not what this is about."

"No," he said. "It's not." He thought of the stars on her forehead, her rumpled face, and how the two of them were the only ones in that group of guests who maybe truly understood failure.

Together, they walked with their arms linked, Dorothy's body curved against him for support. They followed the path around to the front of the house and he opened the car door and helped Dorothy into the front seat. She looked up at him before he shut the door and her face was wet and shining.

A bright moon full of hope.

Cicadas

It was the sound of my window rattling and the moan of the train that scared me awake as a child. I would sit up in bed, bring my knees to my chest, squeeze them tight to my body, and pray to God that the train would move by our house without crashing. My mother said that, right before I was born, a train derailed on the tracks across the road from our house and twenty-four people were killed. She told me the sound of the metal scraping across the tracks stayed in her ears for days, that she couldn't get the noise out of her head. My father said they thought the flames were going to jump across the road and burn the farm and the fields, that's how close the accident was. He said they were lucky it wasn't windy that night and so they got the fire out before it reached our fields. My mother said it was God who spared the farm and I was the reason. God had plans for me, had selected me for some Special Project.

As a child, I was told Jesus watches me, that He is everywhere. I imagined Him floating above my bed, like a giant fish, watching the way I twisted my arm around my pillow as I slept. I wondered if he knew how I dreamt about him, how I imagined him as a fish, or an animal, and not a person. I didn't want him to look like my father. Someone that special, I thought, should have shiny blue-green scales, rounded lips that puckered and puffed, fins that slicked to the side of his body as he swam in and out of the menagerie of rooms in our house.

When my mother found out about my nightmares she told me there was nothing she could do about the sound. She said that when she was afraid of the trains, after the accident, when they finally fixed the tracks and she had to get used to the metallic grind again, the only thing she could do was wait. She said she knew everything was okay when the train finally passed and the only noise left was the rumble in the distance, eventually replaced by the cicadas outside in the field. Once she heard the cicadas she knew everything was all right. She could go back to sleep. It never worked for me, though. I could never hear the cicadas and know I was okay, alone in my room. Unlike my mother, I was left with the imagined sound of Jesus swimming above my bed, slapping at the air, sending waves to the corners of my room.

Eventually, I slept through the trains. It was Rupa Sharma who told me there wouldn't be another accident. Told me I should stop listening to my crazy mother.

"She won't even let you out of the house on Sundays. And that look she gives me, that sideways look? Like she's too afraid to look at me directly? It gives me the creeps."

I was fourteen and believed everything Rupa told me. She was a year older than me and had black hair down to her waist. Hair I envied. When the light hit at just the right angle, strands would light up orange, then disappear again when she would turn her head to say something, as if they were never there in the first place. With her perfectly smooth, wide forehead and dark, round eyes, Rupa, I believed, was the kind of child God would protect.

When I spent the night at her house, her mother would brush my hair after Rupa's, pretending it was as long and thick as her daughter's.

"Next month we'll be able to braid it. Look! It's almost past your shoulders!"

I loved Rupa's mother. Her skin was smooth, the color of caramel candy, and she smelled salty, like the curried rice she made for us on Saturday afternoons.

"She's just a normal mom," Rupa would say, but I knew most mothers wouldn't let you use their make-up, or want you to call them by their first names.

My mother would shake her head when I referred to Rupa's mother by her first name. "She's an adult, Rebecca. Show some respect."

"But she told me to call her Sanja. She says she feels old when I call her Ms. Sharma."

My mother didn't like Sanja Sharma, or Rupa. She called Sanja scandalous, and she did give Rupa looks when she came over to our house. I hated my mother for the way she embarrassed me around Rupa, treating me like a child, making me do chores while Rupa waited quietly in my room for me to finish. I was afraid that—because of my mother—Rupa wouldn't want to be friends anymore. But Rupa didn't care what my mother thought of her. She said she was used to the looks the people in town gave her. Said she'd gotten used to them a long time ago.

"They're just a bunch of damn farmers' wives, anyhow. I can tell you one thing, you wouldn't catch my mother sticking with a lousy farmer." Then she would look at me, and, frowning, would say, "No offense. No, really, you know what I meant."

Sanja Sharma got looks because she lived alone with Rupa and was never married. She had moved here with Rupa because, she said, she needed some space and some quiet for her writing.

When I asked her what she wrote, she laughed and told me she'd let me read one of her books when I got a little older.

Later that night, Rupa sneaked into her mother's room and brought back a book with a bare-chested man on the cover. He held a woman in his arms, and her long dress was torn up to her thigh, her head thrown back with an arm covering her forehead. They stood under a painted tree, their feet covered with mud.

"You can borrow it if you want, she has a bunch of them," Rupa whispered.

"My mom might find it. She'd kill me."

"We can read it here, then. We'll read a little every time you spend the night."

I did want to take the book home and I knew I could hide it from my mother. For some reason, though, I was afraid to have it in my room. I imagined Jesus, floating over my bed, looking down at the couple on the cover, seeing the bare-chested man with the muscles and long, tangled hair, almost kissing the fainting woman. I didn't know what was in the book, what Rupa's mother could have written about these two people that was so bad I had to wait until I was older to read about it. I did know, though, that I wanted Rupa to read it to me here, in her room, with the red flowered wall paper, and the velvet canopy over the bed.

We read the book and giggled, and three others, all with a different bare- chested man and long-haired woman on the cover. Rupa would read in a low voice, walking around the room, moving her free arm through the air dramatically when the couple in the book kissed. She would pause before she got to what she called a nasty scene and say, "Are you ready for this?" We would stay up all night talking about the couple. We didn't know about sex, had only heard stories from some girls at school. I was afraid of the men in the books, the way they moved on top of the women, ripped their clothes off and made noises. I never wanted that to happen to me, I told Rupa. I didn't want someone to get on top of me and rub his chest against my hairless body.

"But that's what happens. That's what everyone does."

"It sounds like it hurts." I watched Rupa put the book in the bottom drawer of her desk, covering it with sheets of paper. She wore one of Sanja's nightgowns; it was short and petal-pink, trimmed with white lace that made her skin look even darker in the dim light of the room. I wore one of my father's old T-shirts, my skinny legs stretching over the end of the bed. I imagined borrowing one of my mother's flannel nightgowns, with the worn elbows and faded flowers.

"It's supposed to feel good." Rupa crawled into bed, pulling the covers up to her chin. "But I'm not stupid. I'm going to wait until I'm married. I'm not even going to let a boy go up my shirt until I've got a ring."

The thought of a man on top of Rupa made my stomach ache. Someone who looked like one of the beasts on the covers of Sanja's books, I thought, could never touch Rupa and not make her hurt.

Rupa got a car when she was sixteen. A cherry red Mustang with a convertible top and enough juice, Rupa said, to beat anyone in town on the strip. Rupa thought about things like that, drag racing and meeting seniors who might take her to prom. She would take me with her some nights and we'd drive around the deserted farm roads looking for the group of older kids who parked their cars in bunches and drank beer in the fields. She wore her hair up in a knot on top of her head when she drove, so the wind wouldn't blow it around and cause it to tangle. She'd pull at the loose strands and steer with her knees while she switched radio stations, the sound of the wind drowning out most of the music. I felt like I didn't belong with her in the car she looked so right in. In my sweatshirt and jeans, my short hair pushed behind my ears, I knew Rupa was the only reason the older kids talked to me. As we drove around looking for headlights, I secretly hoped we would never find the group. I was happy driving in the warm night, the smell of freshly cut fields filling the car, our arms dangling out the open windows.

Rupa would always find the group, though. And she'd climb out of the car, release her hair, say, "Are you ready?" Then she'd walk straight over to the group, leaving me standing next to the car until she came back to get me.

"Loosen up, Rebecca. They're okay." She'd laugh and offer me a beer in a can. I'd take a drink, the warm fullness of it expanding in my stomach, and follow her back to the group. The older girls talked about make-up and parties. They'd look at me out of the corner of their eyes until I felt like I should say something. Usually I couldn't think of anything, so I would nod to show I agreed with whatever they were saying. I didn't know about those things yet. They belonged in Rupa's world, the world she lived in when she wasn't with me.

At sixteen, I had no interest in boys. At least not the boys in the group, who wore their shirt sleeves rolled up to show their muscles and talked about engines and football. I had fallen in what—at the time—I was sure was love with the new preacher at church, the one my mother called "a nice man." I knew I loved him the first day I saw him, when he stood out in front of the church and shook my hand. His skin was slick from the heat, his high forehead perfectly smooth. And the way he touched my hand, tickled my palm with the length of his finger, made me believe my feelings were a sign from God. Not just his touch but the look in his eyes, too. Like God was looking straight at me through this man and asking me to come back to him, to not be afraid of the sound of him.

His name was Mike Walters and he had short blonde hair and a nervous twitch that caused his right eye to blink during the more rigorous parts of his sermon, when he would pound the lectern. I loved the way his face would flush red in the summer heat, when he would stand by the doors of the church, welcoming families on their way in to the service. I would watch him walk up the aisle after shutting the heavy wooden doors, his shirt sleeves rolled up because of the heat. His forearms were thick with blonde hair, his hands wide and strong. When he stood in front of us, behind the lectern, he'd smile. Giving us a look, I assumed, of pride.

He'd had a difficult time at first, because he was young and fresh out of Arlington Baptist Academy. To make people comfortable with him he arranged visits with the families of the church, coming to their houses for early dinners. On the afternoon of his visit to our house I sat up in my room, looking out the window for his car. I wanted to watch the way he pulled up our driveway, got out of his car, walked up to our front door. I imagined him looking up and seeing me through the window. I wanted him to come for me, believed he had arranged these visits as an excuse. Secretly, I hoped he would ask me out onto the porch alone after dinner, where he'd take me in his arms, whisper that I was the girl he'd been waiting for.

Mike Walters came and ate my mother's meat loaf, complimented her on her homemade bread. He talked to my father about the outlook for the crops this year, resting easily on the couch in our living room. I sat across the room and said nothing, waiting for him to give me a secret sign, or a nod, to meet him later outside. His voice was loud and smooth when he talked, when he told us about the seminary school he had attended in Oklahoma City, how he came here because his grandmother was close by, and wasn't it nice and quiet out here? My mother smiled a lot, offered him cookies from a glass dish I had never seen before. He took a handful of the cookies and complimented her on those, too.

"And you," he turned to me, finally, and said, "How do you like growing up here?"

My mother, before I had time to think of something witty and charming, answered for me. "Oh, Becca loves it here. She's very popular in school."

Mike Walters turned to me and smiled. "I don't doubt that at all."

I blushed and turned away in anger.

Rupa was asked to the senior prom by a boy who smelled like fried chicken. His name was Chet Knowles, and he had a cowlick in the front of his hair that made him look like he had a black question mark on the top of his forehead. When I pointed this out to Rupa she looked up from the magazine she was flipping through and glared at me.

"You should be happy for me." She curled a loose strand of hair around a finger. "Look at you, having the hots for some Jesus freak twice your age. Some Baptist bible thumper."

"I don't have the hots for anyone," I lied.

"Oh, come on. He's all you talk about anymore. Don't you think I know why you keep wanting to drive by that stupid church?"

I felt my face go red. "That's just to keep an eye out for my parents. I'm not supposed to be out with you during the week."

Rupa closed the magazine and stared across the table at me, her red nails tapping the top of the formica. "I bet you wish you looked like me so that preacher man would want to get on top of you, get into your pants."

"Shut up." I was mad because she had never said anything more true and I knew then that I would never be able to hide anything from her. I did think Mike Walters would notice me if I had Rupa's hair, her thin waist, her tanned arms.

"And I probably could've gotten Chet to set you up. We could've doubled to prom." She looked away, down the hall. "Mom!" she yelled. "Are you ready yet?" Then, to me, "you still want to come shopping?"

I stood up from the table. "I'm sure you don't need me to find a slutty dress."

"Rebecca," she whined. "Don't be this way."

I walked home through the trees by the creek, thinking about Rupa in a red dress, strapless maybe, dancing with the question mark boy. He would probably tell her how beautiful she looked, how beautiful she was, how nervous she made him. They would kiss in his parents' car afterward when he would try to unzip her dress.

Eventually, Rupa became my friend again. She didn't talk about the prom and when asked she avoided my eyes and looked down at the floor before she said, in almost a whisper, "It wasn't so great." I got my driver's license. My father let me borrow his truck and while Rupa was out in the fields I drove myself by the church on Wednesday nights. I thought of possible date locations to suggest to Mike, in case he happened to wave me over to the side of the road. My ideas included a picnic by my favorite lake, the one on the outskirts of town with the tall sycamores and smell of gardenias. A movie at the old Majestic, with the perfect red velvet couple seats, where the arms lifted to allow better hand holding. Maybe a walk around the fields, where I would wear my favorite skirt, the sky blue one with the stitched white blossoms. I rarely saw Mike, though. And once, when I did see him, I was so embarrassed by it all, the illegal feeling of driving by and spying, that I turned away when he waved and didn't drive by for a long time after that.

Rupa and I were friends again, but not like we were. She stopped asking me to go driving at night and I stopped asking her to the movies. Still, she had me over to spend the night on the weekends. She wanted me to know that she still considered me her best friend.

"Better," she told me, "than any of those stupid cheerleaders I sit with at lunch."

Sanja, too, wanted me to know that I was her daughter's favorite friend. She went out of her way to make my favorite dinners, told me I was welcome over anytime, whether Rupa was home or not. I liked spending time at the Sharma's house; it was more relaxing than my own. I didn't have to worry about my mother looking over my shoulder, asking me when I was going to do the dishes or vacuum the floor in the living room. I was learning to write, too, and Sanja would set up her typewriter for me at the kitchen table, with a pile of fresh, white paper neatly stacked next to it. I was writing poems for my English class. Mostly, they were awful love poems, but Sanja praised them, told me I had a talent for words and should take more classes.

Our junior year Rupa started dating a boy named Trevor. Trevor was tall and thin, with curly red hair he wore long, past his shoulders. He would come to pick Rupa up for their dates in his black Camaro, the stereo up loud enough that the bass pounded through the living room and caused Sanja to yell, "Tell that boy to turn that damn thing down! You'll ruin your ears!"

Rupa would run out to meet him, her long hair falling down her back, her jacket flung over one shoulder.

"I don't like him," Sanja told me one night, after Rupa had been gone past her curfew. "He's the kind of kid that's going to get her in trouble."

I didn't say anything. I didn't like Trevor either; I thought he smelled like B.O. and I hated the way he tried to grow hairs on his chin and upper lip. I ignored him whenever he came over. He didn't like me anyway. He told Rupa I was weird, that she shouldn't even ask him to set me up with one of his friends. I didn't care. He wasn't the kind of guy I'd be interested in, anyway and I imagined a date with one of his friends would go like this: A six pack, a grope up the shirt, a night tipping cows.

Rupa came home from her date an hour late, smelling of beer and cigarettes. When she walked by me, through the kitchen, I thought she'd been crying.

Sanja called her back into her room and I heard them yell. Their voices were muffled. I had to strain and still couldn't hear their words at the other end of the house. When it was over Rupa ran into the kitchen, throwing her jacket onto the table, knocking the stack of paper off the table top.

"I hate her." Rupa's mascara was smeared and her eyes were bloodshot. "I wish she would go to hell."

"She's just worried about you." I bent over to pick up the papers, avoiding Rupa's stare. She bent down next to me.

"You understand, don't you?" She touched my arm; her fingers were cold.

"About what?"

"About how much I love him. You know what it's like."

I grabbed the papers and stood up again, resting my hip against the side of the table. She didn't know anything about the way I felt. There was no way you could feel that strongly about a boy who cursed and wore ripped jeans and I hated Rupa for making the comparison. I knew she was just looking for an ally against her mother. She had never mentioned my feelings before, wasn't interested at all in the way I thought about men.

"I know you like him, Rupa."

"I don't just like him, I'm in love with him." She leaned in close to me. "Can't you understand?"

I told her yes.

Later, we lay in bed, under Rupa's canopy, and she told me about the way Trevor kissed her. "He wants to join the army when he gets out of school. He wants me to come with him." She rubbed the top of the comforter against her chest, her breath smelled now of peppermint toothpaste. "What do you think about that?" she asked me.

"I think you'd better think about it."

She said "good-night," then rolled over onto her side, her back to me. I thought about Trevor in the army, his copper hair shaved short, thin arms white against the green of his uniform. I wanted to tell Rupa she could have so much more, that she could probably have any boy in the world.

That spring my mother got sick. My father had been teasing her about gaining so much weight until she fainted one night on her way to the refrigerator and the doctors removed a tumor the size of a grapefruit that had grown next to her stomach. The house was large and quiet while my mother was in the hospital and my father was out all day bush hogging the fields. I walked through the rooms, touching the furniture. I felt like I was living in someone else's house, with someone else's parents.

Sanja called to let me know she had entered some of my poems in a contest for high school students. "I want you to come over right now!" She said. "I wasn't even going to tell you about it."

On the way over to the Sharma's, I passed my father on the side of the road talking with Mike Walters. Mike had been helping my father mend a fence around the back field, to keep kids from parking their cars there and ruining part of the crop. He'd been finding a lot of broken beer bottles and tire tracks in this part of the field and he was worried about a cigarette maybe catching fire in the dry grass. I slowed down and pulled over to the side of the road. Mike had his shirt off. His chest was wide, stretched tight with muscles. As I got out of the truck, he picked his shirt off the ground and slipped it over his head.

"Rebecca, you don't know the kids that come out here, do you?" My father stepped over to the truck and leaned against it, wiping the sweat from his forehead with the back of his arm.

"Did something happen?"

"Well, there could be a problem if this field catches fire."

The sun was hot on the top of my head; my scalp felt dry, cracked. They were both staring at me, their eyes shifting away from my face when I looked from one to the other. I hated the way my father was talking to me in front of Mike, as if I were a kid. A guilty child.

"Well, maybe Rupa knows something, then. You think you could ask her?" My father put a hand on my shoulder, the skin was rough, it scratched through the thin T-shirt I was wearing.

"She doesn't know, Dad."

My father looked at Mike.

"Your Dad's just worried something's going to happen, Rebecca. Someone could get hurt."

"I'd tell you if I knew something, but I don't, okay?"

I walked around the back of the truck and climbed in behind the steering wheel. My father followed me around. "Where you headed?" he asked.

I thought about telling him the truth. That I'd won the contest and would be leaving this place, these fields. He'd already told me that they didn't have the money to let me go away to school that fall. I'd have to wait at least a year. "The library."

"Could you drop Mike off by his house? I'm going to stay out here a little longer."

I had never been alone with Mike Walters before. He climbed into the seat beside me, his leg resting close to mine on the wide bench seat. I noticed he had a scar on his thigh, above his knee. The whiteness of it cut through the tan of his skin, and I wanted to touch it, feel its smoothness. He saw me look at it and said, "From an accident I had as a kid."

I started the engine and drove slowly down the road. I stared ahead, at the trees in the distance. I could feel Mike's eyes on me and I stretched out my hand to touch his thigh, just next to where the scar was. I laid my hand on his thigh and he let me hold it there until we hit a bump in the road and I pulled back.

"Does it still hurt? When it rains?" I thought of the scar on my mother's side, almost eight inches long is what my father had said.

"Not really," he said. "But I've had it for so long I can't remember not having it, if that makes any sense."

"So maybe you feel something but you're just used to it."

He started to laugh and I turned away from him. I wanted to touch him again. I wanted to let him touch me.

This was the first time I had talked alone with Mike outside the church. Whenever I'd run into him in town, I'd get embarrassed and turn away before he had the chance to come over and say something.

I pulled into the driveway of his house. It was small and needed painting. "Thanks for the ride," he said, shutting the door behind him. "I'll see you Sunday?"

I nodded and watched him walk away, up the dirt path that led to his front door. I wanted to follow him, tell him everything. Instead, I put the truck in reverse and drove out to the Sharma's, feeling as if I'd swallowed a cake whole.

I'd won a contest, Sanja told me, and wasn't it great that they wanted to give me five thousand dollars to help pay college tuition?

"Read the letter, Rebecca!" Sanja slid the envelope to me, across the table. "I know I should've told you, but I didn't want you to get discouraged if you didn't win. We're so proud of you."

Rupa wasn't in the room, but I guessed she was part of the "we" Sanja meant. There was a number I was to call about the paperwork for my scholarship money.

"Why don't we call?" Sanja asked.

"Maybe I should wait." I was afraid that if I called they'd tell me it was a mistake. They'd sent the letter to the wrong person, they were sorry. I didn't want Sanja to find out they'd made an error. She was proud of me; I was her pupil. Her special project.

"Okay." She shrugged. "But you'd better not wait too long, they might give it to someone else." She laughed and stood up from the table. Rupa walked into the room and I thought about what my father had said about the field. I wondered if she went out there with Trevor, thinking my father would never find the bottles. Knowing I would never tell my father that it was her. She smiled at me slowly, her lips painted dark red, the color of wine.

Rupa pulled on my sleeve and I followed her into her bedroom. "I have something to tell you," she whispered. "I'm running away with Trevor."

I held the envelope tight, not wanting to lose it in the mess of her room. She threw things around now, didn't bother with drawers anymore. "You've been saying that for a year now."

"I mean tonight. We're meeting tonight and taking off for good." She bent down and pulled a suitcase from under her bed. "See? We're getting the hell out of this shit hole place." She stood up and kicked the suitcase back under her bed. "It's about time, too."

"Does Sanja know?"

"Are you kidding? She'd kill me. She doesn't understand Trevor." Rupa's voice shook, and when she turned to look at me, she was crying. "Rebecca, you don't know what's happened."

"What do you mean?"

"Oh, you'd never understand. I mean, you're smart. You've got ways out of this place. Not like me." She sat on the bed, crossing her legs.

"If you think Trevor is your only way out of here, you're crazy." I stood and stared down at her, my arms hanging at my sides. I wanted to touch her, brush her hair away from her swollen eyes. "You're not pregnant, are you?" I said this as if it had just occurred to me.

"I don't know." Rupa looked up at me. Her eyes were bloodshot, there were circles underneath them, dark, charcoal half moons. She paused before saying, "No, I'm not."

I touched the top of her crossed hands with my own. "I'll help you," I told her.

"Oh, wake up, Rebecca. Some of us don't need to be helped."

I sat down next to her, under the canopy I loved. I wanted to tell Rupa she was lucky, the canopy had hidden her from Jesus all these years. Under its dark shelter, she was free to do whatever she wanted. Jesus was left in the corner of her room, trying to spy in on her at angles, only seeing what Rupa wanted him to. If I told her this, Rupa would only laugh, though. I believed she had never felt threatened by anyone.

"You don't want me to help?" I asked.

"You can't, really. But I'll write you, I promise. As soon as we're settled."

She took my hand and held it, tracing the veins that stood out on top with the tip of her finger. I felt I should be able to stop her, to protect her. I didn't want her to leave, to run off with a boy who wanted to join the army and drink beer.

I drove to Mike's house without thinking about it. He was out on his porch, his face shadowed from the angle of the sun. As I pulled into his driveway, he looked up from the book he was reading and waved. I stepped out of the truck, my legs weak. I didn't know what I wanted to say to him. I only knew I needed to hear his voice, needed to watch his lips.

"Rebecca," he said as I walked up his steps. "Is anything wrong?"

"No." I was nervous. I handed him the envelope I had carried from the truck.

He took it, "What's this?" He opened it, smiling as he read. "That's great! I didn't know you wrote poetry. I'd like to read some."

"Really?"

"Why not?" He folded the paper and put it back in the envelope.

"Some of them are about you," I said.

He looked surprised, confused. He held the book in front of him, his fingers inside to mark his place. His face was sunburned and I could see the dirt in the creases of his neck. I wanted to tell him everything. I wanted to confess my sins.

"If someone wanted to get away, would you help them?"

Mike stood up and walked to the edge of the porch, his back to me. His shirt was damp with sweat. It was late in the afternoon, and the heat floated through us, filling our lungs with hot dust.

"It would depend on the situation," he said slowly.

"But what if you couldn't stop them?" I needed someone to tell me what to do. I needed Mike to tell me that's what he would do, that's what God would do.

"Rebecca, your mother."

I went to him and put my arms around his waist and held him. I thought of Rupa, of what she would do. I could feel him tense the muscles in his back. He held his arms at his sides until I moved away from him.

He handed back the envelope to me. "You're stronger than you think, Rebecca. There's going to be something big for you in the future." I wanted him to tell me what that was. I wanted to tell him that all the waiting for that something big was killing me, that I wanted something to happen right then, like what was happening to Rupa. But he just stood there, not smiling now, and so I left, thinking about Mike and the house that needed painting. There was Rupa and Trevor, that night, starting something, what? Big? Small? I wished it was me running away with Mike, meeting in a dark field somewhere, nervously putting packed suitcases in the trunk of his car. Driving away to, if not something big, then at least to something. Maybe Rupa was right, this was her way out. I envied her at that moment, thinking that, whatever my future held, I would have traded it for the feel of Mike's hands on my skin. The feel of him pushed up against me, in the backseat of a car, on the side of a road in a place I'd never heard of. I knew I'd never have that. Realized, as I pulled the truck out of Mike's driveway, that I would never be allowed to sneak away in the middle of the night. Responsibility would always swim around me, like Jesus in my room, spying on me while I tried to sleep.

My father woke me up at two in the morning, shaking my shoulder and saying my name. Outside, I heard the train rumble past, the exhale of the horn shaking the window.

"Sanja Sharma is downstairs. She thinks something's happened to Rupa."

Downstairs, Sanja sat on the couch in my parent's living room. She held a glass of water, looking uncomfortable.

Sanja stood up when she noticed me. "Do you know where Rupa is? Did she say anything to you this afternoon?"

I shook my head.

"Rebecca, this is important." My father's voice was scratchy, like he was still half asleep.

"I don't know. She didn't say anything."

Sanja walked over to me, put her arm around my shoulder. "Please, Rebecca, I'm worried."

"Maybe she's just late coming home." My voice did not sound convincing. Sanja's arm felt heavy on my shoulders.

"She's never been this late without calling. I just know something's... I know she's with Trevor."

My father shook his head. Maybe he knew I was lying. Sanja held me closer. I could feel her breath on my neck.

"I don't know," I said quietly. "I don't know where she is." Which was the truth, I didn't know. By then, I figured, they could have been anywhere.

Sanja held me for a minute, quietly. By the way she held her arms around me so tightly, her thin arms almost painful against my back, I could tell that she knew I had finally chosen Rupa. Outside I heard the train, still.

I walked with Sanja out onto the porch, where she held her coat tight around her and started to shake.

"I just know she's with him. I told her." She turned away from me and walked down the steps, to Rupa's car, which was parked in the driveway. In the moonlight, the white convertible top glowed. Before she got in the car she turned and said, "Will you let me know if she's okay?"

I told her I would.

She started the car and drove away, racing the train that ran next to her. I sat and watched the car until it went over a hill and disappeared. I imagined Rupa with Trevor somewhere, driving, in his black Camaro. The stereo turned up loud to keep them both awake. Rupa, lost in the romance of it, on some strange highway, holding Trevor's hand. She hadn't even bothered to ask about my

Mother. She had grown up a long time ago, I realized, and I was just beginning to understand what it took to be an adult.

I was afraid to go back up to my room and so I sat in the dark, pretending I had done the right thing. The train shook the boards of the porch and the rumble went through me and I held my hands over my ears until the train went past. Then, out in the fields, I heard the cicadas. I closed my eyes and waited for the safety that my Mother, upstairs in her bedroom, was maybe waiting for, too. No fire in the fields, no grinding of metal on the tracks, at least not yet.

Laura Kopchick is a graduate of the MFA program in Fiction at the University of Michigan, where she was a Colby Fellow and where she also received a Roy W. Cowden Award in short fiction and a Hopwood Award in short fiction. She is a recipient of the First Place National Award (with a $10,000 prize) in short Fiction from the National Society of Arts and Letters. She currently teaches creative writing at The University of Texas at Arlington and serves as the Coordinator for Creative Writing in the Department of English. From 2007-2015, she served as the Series Editor of the Katherine Anne Porter Prize in short fiction from the University of North Texas Press.

I would like to thank all the wonderful creative writing professors who helped me over the years. I am especially grateful for the ones who became my mentors: Ben Marcus (this book exists because of you), Charles Baxter, Barb Rodman, Ken Harrison, and Janet Peery. I would also like to thank Vicky Santiesteban, Victoria Morrow, and Tim Richardson for being so generous with their feedback on these stories and for also inspiring me with their own writing. You all amaze me. Thanks to Shelley McKinley for being my personal cheerleader. Thanks to all my students, current and past, especially Shaun Hamill. You made me want to be a better teacher. Thanks to my parents, Nick and Sandy, for always supporting me (even after I switched my major to English). Finally, thanks to everyone at Lamar University Literary Press, with a special shout out to Kelsey, who caught every single misused comma.

Printed in the USA
CPSIA information can be obtained
at www.ICGtesting.com
LVHW021612011224
798056LV00046B/744